T[illegible] *ONE*

A[illegible]ring Steve Austin, the Six Million Dollar Man. Books in this series so far include: WINE, WOMEN AND WAR and SOLID GOLD KIDNAPPING, published by Star Books.

SIX MILLION DOLLAR MAN

THE RESCUE OF *ATHENA ONE*

a novel by

Michael Jahn

Based on the Universal Television Series
Created by Martin Caidin

A STAR BOOK
published by
W. H. ALLEN

A Star Book
Published in 1976
by W. H. Allen & Co. Ltd.
A division of Howard & Wyndham Ltd.
44, Hill Street, London W1X 8LB

Published by arrangement with Warner Paperback Library, USA

Printed in Great Britain by
Richard Clay (The Chaucer Press), Ltd., Bungay, Suffolk

ISBN 0 352 39844 2

CHAPTER ONE

The five lights came from the direction of the southern constellation that a nameless ancient astronomer thought looked like a fish and so named Cetus, the Whale. Flying in a rigid formation resembling the points of a star, the lights swept around the dark side of the moon, made several casual orbits of that body, then crossed the 242,000 miles to Earth in half a day. The five lights orbited Earth for a little more than twenty-four hours at the standard orbital velocity of 17,000 miles per hour, watching, thinking, reporting, and glowing with a deep blue fire. At midday on a hot August afternoon, when Cetus, the Whale, was quite invisible, the five lights, then burning a brilliant orange, entered the atmosphere over the continent of North America and began their descent.

The sky over Kennedy Space Center was pure and cloudless, and the sun beat down on KSC's maze of active and inactive launch complexes without letup. The rattlesnakes that normally sunned themselves on the abandoned and cracking concrete pads had slithered off in search of shade, and even the birds had deserted the skies. The Merritt Island National Wildlife Reserve, which is Kennedy Space Center's neighbor to the north, on Merritt Island, inland of the actual Cape Canaveral, was still. Its 134,143 acres was mostly salt marsh, flatlands, tropical woods, which hung limply in the oppressive heat like a drooping sweetgum leaf. All was quiet on Merritt Island, Florida; the best achievements both of man and nature driven to a muttering silence by the ageless beating of the sun.

The heat did not halt activity at Kennedy Space Center, it only made the work barely tolerable. Five years after the last manned lunar mission, work continued at a steady pace on various aspects of the space program. The Space Shuttle had passed its horizontal tests and was less than six months from its first manned, orbital flight. The giant, re-usable rocket stood on pad 39B, one of KSC's two principal launching facilities, waiting for the day when a team of astronauts would lift off in the vehicle's first flight. On the identical pad 39A, a Saturn V rocket stood topped by the *Athena One* command module. That modified *Apollo* capsule, being prepared for imminent launch, was, like the Space Shuttle, part of the effort being expended by the National Aeronautics and Space Administration to make space travel as common as a commuter flight from New York to Boston. *Athena One* was to test certain post-Apollo advancements in guidance and maneuverability, with an eye toward improving man's ability to move at will while in orbit. *Athena One* was also to link up with Skylab B, bringing there an astronomer and a package of solar observation equipment to take advantage of a period of high sunspot activity which might well explain how to better derive energy from the sun. Both the Space Shuttle and the Athena program were part of what NASA had grown fond of calling Spaceport – the effort to turn Kennedy Space Center into man's first commutation port between Earth and the cosmos.

Other activity continued, despite the heat wave. Painters were putting the markings on the gigantic, four-mile-long Shuttle runway, which extended half the length of KSC, from Banana Creek, which bisected the facility, nearly to the wildlife refuge headquarters on Route 402, the boundary between the space center and the refuge. And, adjacent to the TLM-18 telemetry receiving antennas, which received most of the data transmitted to KSC from ascending vehicles, NASA was finishing a 150-foot parabolic transmitting antenna capable of sending high-intensity radio messages from Earth to any point within the solar system. At two little-used and relatively small pads, several American corporations were testing launch vehicles for communications-and-weather satellites.

And, at Launch Complex 13, a lunar Orbiter was being readied for launch. Nominally a NASA project designed to provide information for a highly accurate topographical map of the moon, the probe was also a project of American intelligence, designed to keep an eye on possible Russian landings on the otherwise unscannable far side of the moon. And though work went on at Kennedy Space Center despite the week-long heat wave, the constant beating of the sun was beginning to cause tempers to flare.

One such flare was starting to develop in the Flight Crew Training Building, located in the KSC Industrial Area five miles south of the famous Launch Complex 39, origination point of the Apollo flights. In the Flight Crew Training Building were located the command and lunar-module simulators, computerized mockups of the actual vehicles for use in pilot training. The simulators were always the bane of astronauts. Few crews liked them. Virgil 'Gus' Grissom disliked his *Apollo* simulator so intensely that he once hung a lemon on it. There was only one simulator in use during that hot August afternoon. A gleaming white *Athena* command-module simulator rolled, pitched, and yawed under the influence of its computer brain. Within it, Colonel Steve Austin, astronaut, was losing patience with the command pilot he was training for the imminent *Athena One* mission. Of course, he knew that his temper was related to the heat. Despite the extensive air-conditioning, it was damned hot within that metal box. Still, Commander Wood's lack of cooperation seemed, to Austin, unbearable.

The two astronauts were wearing standard pressure suits, but without their helmets. Instead, they wore light 'Snoopy hoods,' which covered most of their heads, rather like ski masks. The *Athena* command module was, like *Apollo*, a three-seat vehicle. Austin, in the left-hand seat, fiddled angrily with his communicator, listening to the simulated voice of Mission Control come over the small, capsule loudspeaker. Commander Wood, occupying the central position, stared tight-lipped at the gleaming instrument array in front of them.

'*Athena One*, this is Mission Control,' the loudspeaker squawked. 'You are go for correction burn in minus ten.'

'Mission Control, this is *Athena One*,' Austin replied. 'Standing by.'

'Roger. Minus five ... four ... three ... two ... one ... burn.'

Commander Wood pressed a small, square plastic button, then leaned back into the seat. A burn light glowed red for seven seconds, then shut itself off, the simulated burn over.

'*Athena One*,' the loudspeaker said, 'this is Mission Control. Confirm burn completed.'

'Roger, Mission Control.' Austin said. He pushed his communicator away from his lips and turned to the other astronaut.

'Wood, you're flying this thing like you expect the automatic systems to work,' he barked. 'You're not allowing for outside contingencies. You have to be ready to go to manual control at any time.'

Wood nodded reluctantly, as if preferring to believe Austin wasn't there.

'*Athena One*, Kennedy,' Austin said into his microphone.

'Ready for the docking maneuvers when you are.'

'Five by, Steve. What is your distance to the target vehicle?'

'Estimate four miles.'

'Roger, *One*. All systems go ahead for manual docking.'

'Thank you, Mission,' Austin said. 'We're going in.'

Austin tapped the other astronaut on the sleeve. 'Your ball, Major,' he said. He was rewarded with another unconcerned nod. Austin shrugged and began punching information into the on-board computer. Seconds later, a number flashed on a readout screen.

'Two degrees yaw,' Austin said.

Wood grasped the armrest control and fired a short burst on the yaw control jets.

'Too much,' Austin said sharply. 'Bring it back.'

Wood fired another burst, with the result that the attitude-control indicators, three-dimensional compass readouts, began to show the craft wobbling erratically, out of control.

'She's starting to pitch!' Austin yelled, sweat pouring down his forehead, stinging his eyes. 'Bring it back – hard!'

Wood worked furiously at the thruster control.

'Not that way! You'll ...'

The capsule began to buck almost wildly, then suddenly went still. Austin swore loudly and slammed his fist into his armrest. With a metallic screech, the vinyl-and-aluminum armrest caved downward where Austin had hit it, leaving a crater not at all unlike those he had visited on the moon.

'Congratulations, *Athena*,' the capsule loudspeaker announced dryly, 'you're the first victim of gimbal lock.'

'In case you don't know what gimbal lock is, Wood,' Austin said, 'let me fill you in. You have just fixed this capsule so it has no compass, no reference in space. It's just a tin can floating in a very angry sea!'

Paying attention neither to Austin nor his crushed armrest, Major Wood suddenly ripped off the seat belts and pushed open the overhead hatch.

'Where do you think you're going?' Austin yelled.

Wood clambered out of the simulator and jumped to the floor of the flight-simulation room. She tore off her hood, freeing her long brown hair to flutter over her shoulders. She strode angrily away from the capsule, with Austin at her heels.

'I said where do you think you're going, Major?' he said, catching her by the shoulder and spinning her around.

'Out ... Colonel ... sir,' she said, angrily but correctly.

'You run into trouble up there,' Austin said, pointing toward the heavens, 'and you can't walk away from it. Now get back in that capsule and we'll run it again.'

'We've been at this for six hours,' she protested.

'I don't make up the programs, lady. I've just been assigned to help you. And I didn't want to do *that*. Now, do you mind if we go back to work?'

'*Yes sir!*' she snapped, and turned and began to stalk toward the capsule.

'Anything I can do for you?' the voice of Mission Control asked.

'Yeah,' Austin said, 'tell me what I have to do to get fired off this job.' He followed Major Wood back to the simulator, and was stopped when a technician poked his head from the capsule.

'How did you do that?' the technician asked.

'How did I do what?' Austin asked.

'How did you break your left armrest like that?'

'Oh, hell!' Austin said. He had forgotten. 'Look, I'm sorry.'

'What did you do?' Major Wood asked.

'Nothing,' he muttered.

'*How* did you do that?' the technician asked again.

'I've been putting vitamins in my Crunchy Granola,' Austin said.

'Well, you may as well do as Major Wood likes and take a break. When you took out the armrest, you also arced a couple of control circuits. It'll take me an hour or so to fix them.'

'Okay. And sorry.'

'Hey, don't apologize. What am I here for?'

Austin and Wood walked away from the simulator, stripping off their pressure suits as they went.

'An hour, then,' Major Wood said.

'Make it two. No sense getting out of these things just to get in them again.'

'Thanks,' the woman said, and walked off.

Half an hour later, Austin, dressed in a blue polo shirt over white slacks, walked into Launch Control Center. He took the elevator to the second floor, which handled telemetry, tracking, data reduction and evaluation – in short, every aspect of flight control for the growing Spaceport. LCC was housed in a huge room, the walls and ceiling of which were finished in antiseptic, light-green acoustical tiles. There were four rows of work consoles, each with a myriad of dials, switches, buttons, television monitors, and computer readouts. The rows were arranged in concentric circles, the outermost of which bent around a curved wall, its monitors reaching to the ceiling. The innermost row was the smallest. Data was at its most complex and specific in the outermost row; its most simple and general in the innermost. That latter row was, of course, the most important. It was where the operational decisions were made for every NASA launch. At the center of it sat Albert McCall, project director for both *Athena One* and the new Lunar Orbiter. McCall was a middle-aged man who made no pretense of looking otherwise, as did so many tanned men associated with KSC. McCall was pink and pleasantly fat, and possessed of a small, button nose which his glasses were forever sliding down, especially when he was sweating. That week at the Cape, everyone was sweating.

With McCall was Oscar Goldman, a short, wiry man in his mid-forties who loomed very large in many lives, especially Steve Austin's. Goldman was director of the Office of Special Operations, an umbrella organization encompassing the nation's various civilian and military intelligence agencies. As contrasted with McCall, Goldman was neat, tanned, and muscular; a combination of paratrooper, commando, and executive, all of which he had been. Lunar Orbiter Four, just three days from launch, was his brainchild. He was determined to oversee every detail of its construction himself, just as he had done with Steve Austin. He smiled and pushed his chair away from the console when he saw Austin walk into the Launch Control Center.

'Steve, old pal,' he said. 'How's old FIDO doing today?'

'How do you think?' Austin snapped.

'That bad, huh?'

'Worse. That woman could give Euell Gibbons an ulcer.'

'You can't walk out, Steve. Washington specifically asked for you to be flight-dynamics officer on this mission.'

'What do you mean "Washington"? I thought you *were* Washington.'

'Unfortunately, each of us has a superior officer someplace or other.'

'Unfortunately.'

'Besides, Steve, you only have a week to go.'

Austin grimaced, pulled up a chair, and sat down at the console, between Goldman and McCall, who nodded, smiled, and went back to studying a computer readout.

'That's too long by seven days,' Austin said. 'Look, Oscar, I'm not the only astronaut qualified to be FIDO on this project. NASA could assign one of the other –'

'No deal, Steve. The eyes of the world are on this mission.

It's the first flight of an American woman in space. We can't afford to have anything go wrong.'

'So I'm stuck with her. Is that what you're saying?'

'That's it. If it gets any worse, maybe Al and I can figure out something. If Major Wood can't cut it, Al will have to go to the backup pilot. But *you* ride it out, understand?'

'Yeah,' Austin said, 'thanks a heap.'

'Gentlemen, please,' McCall said. 'Let's not have any more talk about backup pilots. Let's just get the damned *Athena* off the ground.'

'And finish the instrument package on Lunar Orbiter,' Goldman said.

'They'll finish it, Oscar,' McCall said. 'Be patient.'

Goldman shrugged, stood up, stretched, and yawned.

'I've got to get some sleep,' he said.

'Why don't you go to your quarters and lie down. Go to sleep for six or eight hours,' Austin suggested.

'You don't think it's bad form for me to duck out now?'

'Are you kidding, Oscar. You've babied this lunar probe along for months. Get a good sleep. Everyone else who can is going to. I am, soon as I discharge my obligations to Washington and The Wonderful Kelly Wood.'

Goldman yawned again, then smiled.

'Well, see you tomorrow.'

'Good night, Oscar.'

'Call me if anything goes wrong.'

'Okay, Oscar,' Austin said, smiling.

Goldman walked from the LCC and stumbled off, half asleep, toward the stairs.

'That man makes me nervous,' McCall said.

'He strikes everybody that way.'

'Oscar treats people like windup toys.'

'Tell me about it,' Austin said dryly.

McCall turned back to his console. Austin rose, surveyed the room idly for a few minutes, then ambled off. A few minutes later he stood on the sidewalk running from the LCC to the Vertical Assembly Building, the 525-foot-high structure, four times the volume of the Statue of Liberty, in which the center's extraterrestrial flights were assembled. It was mid-afternoon. The sun was beginning to describe a path toward the western horizon and, hopefully, an abatement in temperature.

Five miles to the north, Austin could see the outlines of the Merritt Island National Wildlife Refuge. He regretted that, in more than ten years' association with the Cape, he had never gotten to spend much time walking in the refuge. That situation, he thought, would have to be corrected. Austin stepped off the sidewalk and strolled across a long stretch of grass to the bank of Banana Creek. Across the creek, the Shuttle runway shot off into the distance like an eternal ribbon.

Suddenly Austin's attention was diverted to the sky. Standing high above the Cape, in the middle of a perfectly cloudless day, was a formation of five bluish-white lights. Like the points of a star, the lights hovered over pad 39B, perfectly motionless in the August air. Austin stared at them, transfixed. He had seen those lights before; five years before, during the flight home from the moon with *Apollo 17*. That time he dismissed them as being the notorious 'fireflies' – crystallized water droplets – which accompany every astronaut through space. But there they were again, this time hovering motionlessly above Launch Complex 39.

They stayed in position for less than ten seconds, then something seemed to go wrong. The lights shook abruptly, as though torn from within. For an instant they disappeared, then were replaced by a single spherical object about five times the size of the *Athena* service module. Then that object disappeared and was replaced by the lights. Still shaking and unsteady, the lights began moving on an awkward, erratic path to the northwest, over the wildlife refuge. A few seconds later, the lights crashed with a great hiss of steam, out of Austin's view, into the Indian River, that part of the intracoastal waterway which separated the Cape and Merritt Island from mainland Florida.

Austin stared blankly for a moment, then turned and ran into Launch Control Central. He raced to the second floor and collared Al McCall.

'Did you get it on radar?' he asked.

'What?'

'That blaze of lights across the sky!'

'Blaze of light?'

'Just now! A formation of five lights! Didn't you pick it up?'

'Are you serious, Steve?'

'Yes, I'm serious! You mean it didn't show on the radar?'

'Nothing. Not a thing. We watch that screen pretty closely. Look, it happens a lot . . . people see things in the sky.'

'Al . . .'

'It could've been sudden vapor condensation, or something like that. Yeah, it must've been that.'

'Al, it's a hundred ten degrees out there. What the hell is going to condense in that heat?'

'Steve, I don't know,' McCall said, sounding irritated. 'Look, I've got a lot of work to do. And so, by the way, do you. Major Wood is waiting.'

Austin looked at McCall in disbelief. He walked to the radar manager, who had been listening to the conversation.

'Nothing?' Austin asked.

The radar man shrugged apologetically.

'I'm sorry, Steve,' McCall said.

'Forget it,' Austin muttered, and walked off to find a ride back to the Flight Crew Training Building and its ubiquitous Major Wood.

The northwest corner of the Merritt Island National Wildlife Refuge is called Black Point, a mixture of clean sandy beaches and dense salt marshes leading up to a heavily forested area. Off Black Point, the Indian River reaches a width of just over two miles before widening into a wide bay which empties oceanward through the man-made Haulover Canal into a stretch of water aptly named Mosquito Lagoon. The five lights which had come so far from the constellation Cetus, the Whale, rammed into the river and sank beneath forty feet of blackish water. Before the steam cleared and the waves stopped, four figures helped one another onto the sand near Black Point.

There were two older persons: Ilea, a woman, and Keron, a man. With them were two younger travelers, Eymon, a young man, and Minonee, a young woman. All were dressed in bluish-white flight suits made of a metallic fiber. The suits were close-fitting but functional and comfortable. The men's hair was extremely short and brushed forward, close to the skull. The women had longer hair, but brushed straight back. Their skins glistened brightly, as if made of or covered with clear lacquer. Without a word they turned and watched sadly as an underwater explosion rocked their ship and sent a small cloud of white foam spraying into the air. Then the four travelers turned and walked silently across the beach, toward the protection of the woods.

CHAPTER TWO

The travelers walked uneasily along a narrow trail leading through a wide salt marsh. They were fourteen years and 68·4 million million miles from home. They had not spent that much time coming so far just to die on this strangely cold and forbidding planet. But that was exactly the ending that fate offered them. All they could do was the natural thing – stay alive as long as possible and hope for the best. The sun was slipping behind the horizon, and the wildlife refuge was coming alive with odd and frightening sounds.

To the travelers, every sight and sound was a potential enemy. Though they had developed a good working knowledge of Earth's flora and fauna, still the fear of first contact experienced by all aliens was among them. The widgeon-grass, mangrove, and spiny naiad might be poisonous. The brown pelicans and peregrine falcons might be predators. And far off in a bog, the grunting of alligators was terrifying. Worst of all, the coming of nightfall brought the temperature to seventy-five degrees; a temperature which was, for a Cetian, quite chilling. Despite their metal-fiber suits, the four travelers began to shiver.

They quickened their pace and soon reached the relative safety of a small stand of woods. Led by the older of the two men, the group hastened along a dirt trail which wound in a southeast direction, toward the center of the refuge. Minonee, bringing up the rear, hugged her arms close to her body and thought intently.

'We are all frightened,' she said quietly, in English.

No audible response came from her companions. Yet a second later she spoke again. 'Yes, we all are,' she said. 'And we are all cold as well. What shall we do?'

Her companions neither faced her nor spoke. And seconds later she said to them, 'Yes, again you are right. We must find appropriate clothing and something to eat. Then we can find a place to rest while deciding how to go about making contact with the people here.'

Again, there was silence. The four travelers continued along the narrow nature trail until it opened into a large field. The field widened into a stand of perfectly manicured trees arranged in symmetrical rows. It was an orange grove, one of the score of such groves located within the wildlife refuge and leased to private operators. The four travelers walked between the rows, collecting as much fruit as they could carry. A half mile later they came upon a small, brown-shingle farmhouse. Behind it was an old garage, several smaller sheds, and an aging pickup truck. Three of the travelers waited by the truck while Eymon, the young man, walked quietly up to the farmhouse. From the rear porch, a clothesline extended all the way to the garage. On it was hung an assortment of work clothes: brown shirts and khaki pants, and a motley array of socks and gloves.

Eymon stepped silently to the clothesline and yanked from it several pairs of pants and a few shirts. The line snapped back from his fingers, rattling the rusted pulleys which secured it to both house and garage. Suddenly a light flashed on in the farmhouse and the back door was flung open! A man of fifty, wearing an old, plaid cotton robe over droopy nylon pajamas, came rushing into the yard.

'You!' the man yelled. 'What're you doing taking my clothes?'

Eymon stepped back, caught off guard, afraid.

The man in the robe ran toward the Cetian, who began to walk backward, shaking his head as if that gesture would ward off attack.

'I need those things as bad as you do!' the farmer yelled. He backed Eymon against the garage, then reached out and grabbed the Cetian's arm. Instinctively Eymon pushed the man away. Suddenly the old farmer let out a throaty scream! He held his hands up and shook them, trying to force out the pain. Then he crumpled, dead, to the ground.

Eymon stared down at the body in horror, then shifted his attention to his arm, which was throbbing with pain where the man had touched it. He stared intently at his arm, and in a moment the pain abated. He picked up the clothes and began to run. Behind him, a woman's voice could be heard calling for her husband.

'Ed,' the voice yelled, 'what's going on out there, Ed?'

Behind the old truck, Minonee suddenly snapped to attention. 'Eymon is frightened,' she said. 'We must go to him.'

Before she had a chance to move, Eymon had rejoined them. They began to jog back toward the woods.

'Your arm hurts where the man touched you,' she said. 'I'm sorry. Did you have the man hit by an object?'

Eymon made no audible reply, yet Minonee quickly responded, 'But then why did he fall down and cry out in pain?'

The woods eveloped them like a blanket. They stopped jogging and stood for a moment in a small clearing. The sound of crying came from the farmhouse.

'Things are happening that we don't understand,' Minonee said. 'Events have occurred which we didn't anticipate. Apparently, something about our physiology is incompatible with theirs. I should have gone with you to explain, to talk to them. Yes, it is my fault.'

Eymon looked at her with sad eyes. 'Come,' she said,

leading the way. 'We must find a place to hide. Now their authorities will be looking for us.'

Major Kelly Wood was wearing a simple slacks outfit designed to show her femininity without getting pushy about it. She stood in the shadows backstage at a television studio in Orlando, waiting to make an obligatory talk-show appearance. With her was Steve Austin, who wore a tan summer suit cut along fairly conservative lines. She was beautiful; he, a muscular and tanned six-footer, resembled nothing so much as a Miami Dolphins quarterback. Together they made an outstanding pair. It was unfortunate, Austin thought, that they couldn't stand each other.

Austin, having been the last man to walk on the moon, was, like the other *Apollo* astronauts, still quite a celebrity. This was especially true in the area of Florida surrounding Kennedy Space Center. Austin could barely go outside without being asked for his autograph. Even backstage at the TV studio he was obliged to sign this or that for several station secretaries, a fact which irked Major Wood.

'Well, the colonel seems to have a lot of friends here, too,' she said caustically.

'Major, in case you don't remember, I did spend some time at the center a couple of years ago.'

'Oh, I remember.'

'Look, we don't have to get alone,' Austin said. 'As far as I'm concerned, all you have to do is check out perfectly in that simulator. Then, if you pardon the expression, up you go.'

'Very good, sir.'

'One other thing, Major. We have to make this TV appearance. So how about a truce ... for the sake of the mission.'

'You do your job,' she said, 'I'll do mine. Sir.'

She turned away from Austin and followed the signal of

an aide who was directing the pair to take seats on either side of a scholarly looking man of forty named Jules Bergman. The lights were unbearably hot, reminding Austin of the miserable day spent boiling in the *Athena* simulator. An aide clipped a lavoliere microphone onto Austin's lapel and arranged another for Major Wood. Telemetry sensors, Austin thought. These days everyone has a device of some kind they want to glue on your skin or plug into you in some fashion. Behind two large cameras on dollies, a man with a clipboard was waving his fingers at Bergman.

'Tonight, ladies and gentlemen,' the man announced, 'we are pleased to have a brief interview with two persons crucial to operations at Kennedy Space Center. With me in the studio are Major Kelly Wood and Colonel Steve Austin. Steve, it's good to see you again.'

'Thanks, Jules,' Austin said uncomfortably.

'Major Wood, it's good to meet you. Of course, we all know that you will be the first American woman in space. It's a great honor having you here with us tonight.'

'Thank you,' Major Wood said. 'My copilot, Major Osterman, had to stay at the Cape; otherwise he would be here with me.'

'Just to fill in the background a little,' Bergman said, 'Steve Austin has been with the space program for over a decade. He was the command pilot on *Apollo 17*, and was the last man to set foot on the surface of the moon. Since no manned missions are planned for a long time – perhaps not until the end of the century – that is quite a significant achievement. Steve had a bad accident a few years ago while testing a prototype of the Space Shuttle, from which he obviously has recovered in full. Steve, I understand the Space Shuttle has recovered as well.'

'It certainly has,' Austin said. 'We worked out the bugs in the various prototypes, and now have a Shuttle we're very happy with. It's ready to go. It could go at any time, but isn't scheduled for its first manned, orbital flight until early next year. It's just sitting there. Want to go for a ride, Jules.'

'I'm afraid I'm not the type,' the host said. 'I get airsick in an elevator. Major Wood is much more suited for that sort of adventure. She is an Air Force nurse, served under fire in Vietnam for a number of years, flying medical evacuation helicopters. After the American pullout, she became the first woman test pilot to fly military equipment, and was a natural for selection as the first American woman astronaut. Major, how do you feel about the fact that you will be flying with a male astronaut?'

'Well, let's face it,' she said. 'Every American astronaut to date has been a man. They've had the most experience in space. I suppose women will just have to make their own mark. But I do think we could have gone with two women on *Athena One*.'

'Steve, any opinion on that?'

'There's no doubt that women check out as good as men on the ground, and I'm sure they'll do fine in space,' Austin said. 'But that's not the problem.'

'Then what is?'

'This is a dangerous business we're in. Despite nearly fifteen years' experience in space, man is still an alien there. Our ships are far from perfect. They are safe . . . if handled properly and if no accidents occur. We all know that, and we live with it every day, every time one of us goes up. And we fight to avoid accidents. We don't want to lose anyone up there, Jules, certainly not someone as special as Major Wood.'

'Are you suggesting that *Athena One* is a dangerous mission?'

'They're all dangerous. *Athena One* is like all the others. It's a hostile world up there. If you sail a boat and fall overboard, you can swim. If you fall out of an airplane, you might have a parachute. If your car goes out of control, you have time to do something about it. In space, there's no grace period. If you are exposed to the vacuum of space, you perish instantly. That's why we're so careful.'

'You know, Colonel,' Bergman said, 'that's the first time I've heard you express concern about accidents. Most astronauts don't even admit the possibility. Major Wood, have you considered the possibility of such an accident?'

'Yes,' she said uncertainly, distracted by the compliment paid her by Austin. 'There is always that possibility.'

'Still, we survived *Gemini VIII*, when Armstrong and Scott had to make an emergency landing in the Pacific,' Austin said. 'And we survived *Apollo 13*, when an explosion blew out an entire panel in the service module. We got them back in good shape, and we'll do the same thing with *Athena One*. It's my job to make sure that all runs smoothly. We can't be too complacent about space. One of the missions of *Athena One* is to teach us how to be more secure up there. I know Major Wood will fly a perfect mission.'

'Well,' Bergman said, 'thank you both. I know you have to hurry back to the Cape. We'll be following you on television, Major.'

'Thank you,' she said quietly. Bergman introduced a commercial, an aide removed their microphones, and the two astronauts walked offstage.

'That wasn't so bad, was it?' Austin said.

Major Wood smiled. 'No,' she said, 'and the best part was getting to see the other side of Colonel Steve Austin.'

'Major, I know it's hard for you to understand,' Austin said, 'but when I'm rough on you in that simulator, it has nothing to do with you personally.'

Major Wood stopped, turned to Austin, and studied his face intently. 'I know that,' she said quietly. 'I *do* know that.'

The two astronauts smiled warmly at each other and Austin gently squeezed her shoulder. She turned toward the exit and walked into one support of a high parallel platform. Two workmen atop the platform yelled, Major Wood toppled to her back on the floor, then watched in mute horror as a six-hundred-pound Ten-K lamp rolled off the swaying platform and plummeted straight down at her! Austin jumped quickly to a position straddling the fallen astronaut! He caught the lamp in his left hand, stopping its downward motion just inches short of the point where it otherwise would have crushed her chest. With a modest grunt, he set the lamp on the floor.

'Hey, you okay down there?' one workman called.

'It missed us by a mile,' Austin replied. The two men exchanged bewildered stares. Austin helped the woman to her feet and urged her toward the studio door.

'Steve, those lights weigh a ton,' she said, still shaking with fear and disbelief.

'They do?' he said ingenuously.

'And you caught it in one hand. How?'

'Two hands are for beginners.'

The exit from the backstage area to the parking lot was a heavy-machinery bay with a large sliding steel door. Austin pushed it open effortlessly.

'You can open doors for me *anytime*, Colonel,' the woman said. 'Now, I want to know what's going on.'

'Kelly . . .' Austin said pleadingly.

'No dice. Don't think you can get around me by suddenly being friendly. Either you tell me how you did that or I'll ask everyone at NASA until I find someone who will.'

'Nobody there knows,' Austin said tersely.

'Then I'll try your precious Mr Goldman.'

'Major Wood,' Austin said angrily, 'have you ever heard of something called security clearance?'

'I've heard,' she said, 'I have a five.'

'I have a six. And that's what you'll need.'

'Steve, if you don't tell me, I'm going to throw such a tantrum the whole goddamn base will know by morning. What good will a security clearance six do if everybody knows you can catch a lamp weighing a ton in one hand.'

'You wouldn't do that. It would ruin your career.'

'Of course it would. But it would also wreck yours, I'm willing to bet. Now, are you prepared to blow two perfectly good careers just for the sake of one crummy secret?'

'That crummy secret cost six million dollars.'

'What cost six million dollars?'

'I did.'

'I don't understand.'

'Let's go back to my house and have a drink,' Austin said, pushing her toward his car. 'I think you'd better be sitting down for this one.'

CHAPTER THREE

Steve Austin was a cyborg, a perfect amalgam of man and machine wrenched by science from the jaws of a tragic accident. He could run faster than any man – well over sixty miles per hour, and he could maintain that pace indefinitely. He could lift more than a thousand pounds with one arm and, using all his strength, more than thirty-five hundred pounds. He could jump straight up higher than three stories into the air, and swim at better than thirty-five knots – as fast as a dolphin. And those limits were not absolute. He simply had never pushed himself further. He was, in fact, somewhat frightened by the prospect of ever finding out just what his limits were, so he never did.

Austin's career started normally enough, though in retrospect it seemed that everything was preparing him to be the most unique man in history. Since childhood, his main passion was flying. As soon as he was old enough he took lessons and became a qualified pilot. In college he earned three master's degrees, in aerodynamics, astronautical engineering, and history. While in school Austin became involved in a rigorous program of physical fitness, earning black belts in judo and aikido.

After college he entered the Army to learn to fly a helicopter, and piloted a gunship in Vietnam for a year. Shot down amid a jungle firefight, Austin found himself with a minor wound and a ticket back to the United States. By then it was the mid-1960s, and NASA had just begun its much-heralded Apollo program, which one day was to carry men to the moon. Austin transferred to the Air Force, and before long was into the astronaut training program. On the route, he picked up a lot of test-pilot experience, favoring exotic vehicles like the SR-71, a thin jet which cruised twenty miles up at two thousand miles per hour, and the various early 'lifting bodies,' wingless vehicles designed to be fired into space by conventional rockets, then cruise to an airstrip landing, deriving lift from the shape of the hull alone.

Austin was selected for the Apollo program too late for the early flights. He was designed to be the backup pilot for *Apollo 17*, the final lunar mission, budget considerations having forced the cancellation of *Apollos 18* and *19*. Two weeks before the scheduled liftoff, the mission commander broke his arm in a car accident, moving Air Force Colonel Steve Austin into the pilot's seat. In a way, the accident was fortuitous. Austin, with his considerable scientific background, was really a better choice for *Apollo 17* than his luckless predecessor. Since *Apollos 18* and *19* were canceled, many of the scientific experiments due to be carried out in them were crammed into *Apollo 17*, and Austin's presence proved a vital asset. *Apollo 17* lifted off at 12:33 A.M. the morning of 7 December 1972. The Saturn V vehicle with its human payload, 360 feet tall in all, burned with a flame so brilliant that it washed out all searchlights, bathed Kennedy Space Center in a light approximating daylight, and could be seen as far north as Georgia. When it was completed, *Apollo 17* was considered the most successful of the lunar missions. It set ten records, including longest single moonwalk, Austin's seven hours and thirty-seven minutes.

When *Apollo 17* returned to Earth at 2:24 P.M. on 17 December, near the carrier *Ticonderoga*, Dr Kurt H. Debus, director of KSC, commented that '*Apollo 17* was a glorious conclusion to a program which gave the nation the capability to solve its problems.' The crew went on a nationwide tour and, when all the shouting died down, Steve Austin returned to the life of a test pilot. He turned down numerous offers of high-paying positions in private industry, as he declined invitations to endorse or otherwise advertise products ranging from spacecraft to microwave ovens. His main love was flying, and fly he was determined to do. He accepted an invitation to test fly the M3F5 lifting body.

The M3F5 was a nasty little creation which no pilot liked. But it was a precursor to the Space Shuttle, and that was the next phase of the American space program. If KSC was to become a 'Spaceport,' if indeed there was to be a Spaceport at all, a reusable space vehicle would have to be designed. Once such a ship existed and was operational, a permanent space station could easily be constructed, perhaps around the already-existing Skylab. Men could come and go from Earth to space with relative ease and freedom. Clearly, the M3F5 had to be tested, no matter how nasty it was. It was a question of duty. Steve Austin saw that duty and accepted it. The day he strapped himself into the craft, he set into motion the incredible chain of events that were to make him the world's first bionic man.

The wingless silver dart rode into the sky attached to the left underwing of a giant B-52 bomber. At 45,000 feet, Austin fired the explosive bolts which freed his craft from its tender. Its nose up forty-five degrees, the M3F5 dropped 3,000 feet when Austin pushed the throttle forward into ignition phase. The huge, liquid-hydrogen rocket, similar to the main engine on the lunar module, blasted Austin back into his seat. He pulled back slightly on the stick, and the nose lifted to an angle of seventy degrees. The roar of the engine was far behind him as the slender vessel spread shock waves across the western landscape. Austin brought the nose down at 280,000 feet. The sky had disappeared. There was no blue, only the blackness of space. Beneath him, Earth's horizon curved away sharply, like a brilliant blue-and-white ball. Austin shut down the main engine. The M3F5 soared to 328,000 feet, more than sixty miles high. Austin hit the nitrogen-pressure switch, which flooded the fuel tanks and vented what remained of the highly volatile propellant. For a moment he indulged in sightseeing. His sunblindness had left him, and Austin could see the stars which had become familiar guideposts for him over the years.

The horizon began to flatten. The M3F5 entered the atmosphere belly first, the heat shielding on that part of the hull absorbing the extreme friction of re-entry. That type of re-entry was much trickier than the usual command module re-entry. In the latter case, a standard ballistic approach augmented in the final stages with parachutes sufficed. But Austin's M3F5 had to function both as spacecraft *and* airplane. It had to re-enter like a spacecraft, but land as an airplane. It was a dangerous game he was playing. But it was the only game in town, if a space shuttle was ever to be developed.

The M3F5 was shaped like an elongated bathtub, with three small stabilizing fins attached to the aft end. Austin had to keep the nose positioned just right, or the buffeting of re-entry, especially during the transition from super to subsonic flight, would rip the craft apart. The re-entry was terrifying. Bits and pieces of heat shielding burned off and flew past the cockpit window with a bright orange glow. The M3F5 began to yaw, its nose rolling from side to side. Austin worked the controls and clenched his teeth. The radio was abuzz with nervous queries from the two chase craft assigned to keep an eye on him. Austin felt his hand creep to the button that would eject him to the safety of a parachute. No, he thought, he had never lost one before, and it was not the time to start.

The long expanse of the NASA facility at Rogers Dry Lake, California, rose to meet him, too fast, too fast. The chase pilots were screaming. There was a loud bang, and Austin's head slammed into the side of the cockpit. One wheel dug into the runway and tore off. The M3F5 began to roll, somersault, and break up, spewing debris and liquids into the desert air. It was over in a minute, and all that could be heard were sirens and an occasional sob.

When they pulled him from that wreck, Steve Austin was a man barely alive. He had lost both legs and his left arm. His left eye was gone, ripped out by the same pieee of flying metal which had shattered several ribs and damaged a heart valve. Austin's jaw was crushed and most of his teeth were missing. His skull was fractured, and there were shards of skin hanging uselessly from his torso. But his burns were minor, and the femoral arteries had clamped shut during the wrenching forces of the crash. He would live, though those persons closest to him prayed fervently that he would not. The alternative to death would seem to be a life-time spent as a 'basket case.'

But that was before any of them heard of Oscar Goldman. For years Goldman had been waiting for such a moment. He was head of the most powerful intelligence operation in the West, and had a great deal of money to spend on what he called 'special projects.' The most esoteric of those special projects was the creating of the world's first bionic man.

Bionics was a new science, less than a decade and a half old when Austin had his accident. The word *bionic* derived from Greek roots meaning 'in a manner approximating life.' Bionics was, in a sense, the highest tribute to the abilities of evolution. Bionic scientists realized that never had there been an instrument more efficient for use in grasping and manipulating than the human hand, with its fingers and opposing thumb. Never had there been invented a temperature-regulation device as finely tuned as that found in the higher mammals. Bionic scientists made it their work to create mechanical and electronic devices which duplicated the actions of natural devices. And though the idea sounded fanciful, it was quite logical. The fact that a human hand works is ample proof that a properly constructed artificial hand will also work. The key phrase is *properly constructed*. When it first developed in the late 1950s, bionics concerned itself with little more than the production of crude artificial limbs. But before long, the science grew to include such disciplines as biology, medicine, cybernetics, information theory, and mechanical, electrical, and nuclear engineering. By the dawn of the 1970s, scientists at the Bionics Research Laboratory had the ability to produce a bionic man. The crash of the M3F5 in 1973 brought them the man. Oscar Goldman brought the money.

There was little excuse for a purely research facility such as BRL to spend a great deal of money on one Steve Austin just to prove that it could be done. The nation's veterans' hospitals were already crowded with multiple amputees, many of whom would have eagerly accepted the chance to walk again. But Steve Austin was special. He was an Air Force colonel with a great deal of flight training. He was an astronaut and a celebrity. He had a perfect cover for a covert operation. He was a scientist in his own right, and not only a scientist but an expert on rockets and other military systems. And he was already accustomed to a certain physical prowess. Clearly, Steve Austin was the ideal subject.

Austin was flown to the Bionics Research Laboratory, hacked out of the eastern face of the Rocky Mountains just north of Denver, Colorado. where the forces of science and government were marshaling. The bionic engineers would repair him; would, in fact, make him better than he had been. Oscar Goldman would put in their hands the sum of six million dollars with which to do it. And, when the work was completed, Steve Austin would devote his newfound energies to the work of the Office of Strategic Operations, as America's newest and most exotic secret weapon. Dr Rudy Wells, chief medical officer on the project, could hardly say no. The alternative was, for Austin, too frightful to imagine.

Wells kept Austin unconscious for weeks, using an electrosleep process pioneered, ironically, by Russian doctors. By thus manipulating the astronaut's brain waves, the doctor could perform extensive surgery without running the risks inherent when conventional anesthetics are used for extended periods. Austin's torn heart valve was replaced by an artificial one. The fractured part of his skull was removed and replaced by a plate made of cesium, an alkali metal light and strong yet cabable of withstanding a blow ten times what it would normally take to crush bone. Austin's ribs were replaced with ribs fabricated of vitallium, joined one to the other with artificial tendons. The entire rib cage was extra-joined to the breastbone with silastic, a variant of silicone rubber. The metal ribs were embedded with fine wires, forming an excellent radio antenna.

Austin's jaw was repaired with appropriate applications of metal, ceramics, and plastic. New teeth, made of nylon, were installed. The left eye was replaced at first with a miniature camera built into an artificial eyeball. Later, when advances in microcircuitry and neurology permitted, the camera eye was removed and replaced by an actual, working bionic eye. The principle was the same used for decades in military and astronomical applications – the photomultiplier tube. That was a device not unlike a television camera, in which a series of sensitive plates were used to magnify light energy. With his bionic eye, Austin could not only see, he could see in the dark. The bionic eye incorporated a 20-power zoom lens activated by will, as well as the photomultiplier element, which allowed light amplification by a factor of ten million.

And there were the three bionic limbs; Austin's two legs and his left arm. To the arm and leg stumps Rudy Wells attached bones made of a stainless alloy. The attachment points, as well as key, undamaged natural bone points throughout Austin's body, were reinforced with alloy in order to allow the extra strength imparted by the limbs. Actual nerves and muscle were attached to bionic nerves and muscle, the natural nerve impulses amplified to bionic levels by a maze of sensors and generators. Each limb had a miniature nuclear generator creating heat which was then transformed into electrical energy by a thermopile. Each limb had thousands of sensors duplicating the touch and temperature-sensing nerves of an actual human limb. These sensors fed impulses into servomechanisms which allowed Austin to apply just as much force as was needed for a certain task. Whether the task was breaking down a concrete wall or lifting a teacup, Austin could do it naturally, without thinking about it, as is done by a natural limb. Each limb had an elaborate mechanical structure which duplicated exactly the actions of its human counterpart. The entire array was run by three miniaturized computers, one for each limb. Surrounding the mechanism was a sheath of alloy, sponge, and plastiskin designed to duplicate the form of Austin's natural limbs. Excess heat from the generators was used to simulate normal skin temperature. Hairs were embedded in the plastiskin, which also received a photochemical dye treatment allowing it to tan somewhat when exposed to the sun. When the bionic transformation was complete, all Austin was unable to do was cut his nails.

In the interests of Austin's projected future with the Office of Strategic Operations (OSO), there added a few more improvements. Built into the bottom of each foot was a plastiskin flap hiding foldout swim fins fabricated of woven stainless steel. A similar self-sealing plastikin seam in the thigh of his right leg contained a weapons compartment. While it could contain any number of things, the usual equipment included a compressed air tank with folding face mask, mouthpiece, and breathing tube, and a microminiature radio transmitter with the capability of burst-transmitting previously recorded messages. The final piece of OSO innovation was in the middle finger of Austin's left hand: a CO_2-powered dart gun firing six darts from a revolving chamber when Austin pressed a hidden button with his thumb. The darts were poison-tipped and killed within six seconds of penetration.

The transformation of Steve Austin into the world's first bionic man took close to a year. For fully half that time Austin had little awareness of what was happening. The necessity of intense electrosleep precluded that. And, on the few occasions when he was awake enough to be talked to, Austin either didn't understand the enormity of the circumstance fate had thrust him into, or else refused to believe it. Until he actually tried his bionic equipment, Austin thought all he was getting were classy prosthetic devices, super wooden legs. Another problem grew out of Austin's lack of participation in the plans for his own transformation. At first he was furious. He had, as Oscar Goldman euphemistically put it, 'a problem of emotional adjustment.' Nearly all his life Steve Austin had been free; enjoyed the sensation of flying; the thrill of looking back on the blue-and-white globe called Earth. He had followed his own path, and would have preferred to follow it to its ultimate conclusion, even if that was death in the wreckage of the M3F5.

Instead, he found himself a prisoner of the American intelligence establishment. Not that he was morally opposed to OSO; quite the contrary. Austin simply resented being put on call for the rest of his life. Never knowing when he would be whisked off to some Godforsaken corner of the globe to perform some 'mission' for Oscar Goldman. Had he chosen that path, all would have been fine. But the path was chosen for him, while he was unconscious. And the choosers expended much effort to put him back together – a year's work and six million dollars. He *owed* them. They gave him back his life. Perhaps, he thought, he could justify his tenure with OSO as a form of paying the doctor's bill. And he *was* a good Air Force officer. Before long, he made his 'emotional adjustment.' After a while, when the bionic equipment became natural to him, he began to like it.

Austin gazed out the the window of his one-bedroom apartment in the astronauts' quarters on the top floor of KSC's Manned Spacecraft Operations Building. It was close to midnight, and the searchlights illuminating the Saturn V rocket and its *Athena* payload were out. The sky was still cloudless and, by cupping his hand over his eyes and pressing his face against the glass, he could see Jupiter shining in the constellation Capricorn. A full moon obscured the rest of the sky. Austin let out a deep sigh, then looked down when a hand snaked around him and pressed a drink against his chest.

'What's this?' he asked.

'A cactus cooler,' Kelly Wood said. 'I don't know, I'm no bartender. It's vodka and whatever that juice was you had in the ice box.'

'Thanks,' he said, sipping it. He turned to face her.

'That's an incredible story,' she said softly.

'Well, I make it a little bit more grim than it is. I'm pretty much over the bad parts. I fly when I want to. God knows, I might even get back in space someday.'

'You will. I know it.'

'Ah,' Austin shrugged.

'Colonel ... Steve ... I don't want to see you turn into a quitter.'

'Who's a quitter?' Austin said, bolting down his drink. 'I'm no quitter. I'm a Buick. A supercharged one.'

She laughed, and Austin hugged her and kissed her forehead. 'Back to your quarters, Major,' he said. 'You've got to get some sleep while you can.' He turned her around and walked her to the door.

Major Wood reached into her bag and withdrew a set of keys. She dropped them in Austin's palm. 'Spare set,' she said. 'Do you know how to feed angel fish?'

'I think I can manage.'

'Good. Tomorrow I have to go away for a few days.'

When she was gone, Austin made himself another vodka, then took off his shoes, loosened his shirt, turned off all the lights, and sat down by the window to gaze at the moon and dream.

CHAPTER FOUR

The four Cetians spent a restless and worrisome night hidden in an especially thick stand of exotic Australian pine. Sounds of the terrestrial wildlife, a thousand times more clamorous than the Cetian fauna, assaulted from all directions their extraordinarily responsive senses. A scrub jay scolded them loudly for camping near its nest, and, much to their horror, an old and friendly raccoon had decided, with more wisdom than he ever knew, that the group of hominoids was endlessly interesting. He nosed around their encampment for half an hour, terrifying them thoroughly. But the first rays of dawn drove him back to his nest, and from that point on, the only visitor was a middle-aged box turtle who amused the Cetians with a display of toadstool-eating.

But the amusement was short-lived. Eymon was sick. The pain he had felt when the farmer whose clothing he took touched him was back, and had spread all over his arm. The discomfort had become so great that even the considerable ability to alter objects and events given by evolution to Cetians was unable to ease it. When Ed Hermon first touched him, Eymon was able to will away the pain. But after three or four hours the pain returned, and by morning had become so potent as to make him weak, frightened, and nauseous. Whatever the affliction was, it was spreading to his entire body, and he knew that by evening it would consume him. This worried him even more than one might be expected to worry over one's own death, as it was his job to protect his family. Without him they would be virtually hopeless. The others knew these things, and together discussed the situation, sitting in the reverent silence in which all Cetian groups communicated. Finally, Minonee rose and brushed the pine needles from her clothes.

'We must make our way to the Space Center on foot,' she said in English that carried, most remarkably, the slightest trace of West End London. 'If we are to survive, it will be through that installation. We will find people there who will understand out situation. But we must be careful to avoid detection on the way. I am afraid that the death of the fruitgrower will be interpreted by local residents as a simple, terrestrial crime. I am afraid too that since our credentials have disappeared beneath the waters of that lagoon, our tale might not be sympathetically received by the local authorities. And, of course, it is imperative that we do not touch them or allow them to touch us. Apparently, when a Cetian touches a Terran, the death of both is inevitable. We all share Eymon's agony. Now, let us go.'

'What shall we do with the dead man's clothing?' Eymon asked in Cetian, a glottal language which contained sufficient consonants to choke a Welshman.

'Leave them,' she replied. 'They proved to be of no use to us. Our frames are much smaller than theirs.'

Minonee's mother, brother, and sister stood and brushed off their flight suits. With Minonee in the lead, they started to walk in a southerly direction, toward the junction of the wildlife refuge and the Kennedy Space Center. They had traveled but a half-dozen paces when Eymon stopped them.

They shared thoughts for a few moments, then Minonee nodded and smiled. 'It is a good idea,' she said. 'Bring the clothes along. Perhaps we can use them later for a diversion.' Eymon retrieved the clothes, tied them into a tight bundle, and the group started once again through the forest.

A series of dikes described two thirds of a circle parallel to the shore of the Indian River near Black Point and about a mile inshore from it. The four travelers walked slowly along this dike, figuring, correctly, that sooner or later it would bring them to civilization. The going was slow. The region was thick with freshwater marshes, and trails were few. Many times the Cetians found themselves walking in circles, and more than once one or another of them nearly tumbled into a patch of thick black mud. But the day was warming, and by noon the temperature had reached one hundred degrees, just within the range a Cetian would consider respectable. And the travelers were becoming accustomed somewhat to terrestrial animals – the small ones at least. Birds no longer bothered them, and they had the good fortune not to encounter an alligator, though that species abounded in the array of streams and ponds they skirted.

Still, the air was a good deal thicker than the atmosphere to which they were accustomed. The additional oxygen caused them to hyperventilate, and hence they became dizzy with even the slightest exertion. They could walk no longer than fifteen minutes before having to rest another fifteen minutes. Because of this, and because of the roughness of the terrain, the two miles from where they camped to the junction of routes 402 and 406 took them all morning and left them exhausted.

Routes 402 and 406 are the main highways traversing the wildlife refuge, the former also serving as the boundary with the Space Center. From mainland Florida, one who wishes to visit the wildlife refuge or the ocean might take Route 406 through Titusville, across a short bridge spanning Indian River. Shortly after entering the refuge, 406 sprouts a branch, 402, which leads directly east to Playalinda Beach. That is the location where millions of tourists and space-buffs gather to watch launches. On that hot August day, 402 was jammed with cars, all trying to get to the beach, find a parking spot, and ultimately watch the launch of *Athena One*, scheduled for late that night. It was only NASA's second night launch, the first one, coincidentally, being Austin's *Apollo 17*. For the tourists, night launches were the ultimate space spectacle, and a great many of them were making for the beach, honking their horns, swearing at one another, and crawling at a snail's pace through the sweltering heat.

The four Cetians emerged from the woods just east of the junction of 402 and 406. Careful to stay hidden, they worked their way through the roadside bushes to the fork in the two highways. The line of cars curving from 406 to 402 stood out like a band of colored steel, a hundred yards away.

'Where do you suppose they're going?' Eymon asked in Cetian.

'I don't know.' Minonee said. 'Perhaps to view the Terrans' upcoming launch.'

'We can use one of these vehicles as a diversion,' he said.

'How do you mean?'

'I can put the Terran clothes in one of them.'

'Yes, Then, if the authorities find the clothes, they will take time to question the occupants of the vehicle. It may give us the chance to reach the Space Center undetected.'

'But will it not cause the occupants of the vehicle to be blamed for the death of that farmer?'

'I do not think so.' Minonee said. 'Certainly, he or she will have been identifiable elsewhere at the time. And, of course, the clothes will have traces of us . . . our skin, perhaps. No, they will be inconvenienced, but that is a small price to pay for the success of our mission.'

'I agree,' Eymon said. With that, he dropped the bundle of clothes onto the ground in front of him.

'That one,' Minonee said, pointing out a blue Ford pickup truck, 'the one with the open section. Put the clothes in the back.'

Eymon pointed at the bundle of clothes, then raised his finger to point at the truck, which was slowed, like everyone else, by the incredible traffic. Swiftly, as if propelled by an invisible rocket, the tightly tied bundle flew through the air, curved over the road, and dropped into the back of the pickup. The clothing undetected by the passengers, the truck moved quietly down the road toward Playalinda Beach.

Eymon and Minonee returned to the forest with their parents. The four travelers pushed and stumbled their way through the thick vegetation, working along Route 406, looking for a place to rest and wait for a chance to cross the automobile-choked road. Before long they came to a newly paved single-lane road leading north from 406 to a spit which extended halfway across Indian River. The road, constructed for the use of rangers and refuge maintenance personnel, was closed to the public. The travelers walked northward on it until they came to a spot where the road crossed a large culvert which was, at the time, dry. The group entered the culvert and sat against the wall, to eat oranges and rest.

Austin woke at seven, washed and dressed quickly, and breakfasted with Major Wood in the astronaut's commissary. Out of deference to her, Austin forswore his usual bacon and eggs and joined her in partaking of the unfortunate culinary necessity which NASA euphemistically termed the 'low-residue diet.' The steak and eggs contained an admirable portion of protein, but undiluted by such normal comestibles as bread and milk, it sat in the stomach rather like a softball. Major Wood hated it, but out of duty, not to mention propriety, she complied.

After the meal the two astronauts trekked to the Flight Crew Training Building, suited up, and spent a surprisingly pleasant morning completing the simulator training. The morning was pleasant for several reasons. The first was mundane but important – the air-conditioning worked. The second was quite important indeed. Kelly Wood checked out perfectly on the simulator, performing exactly several functions which had eluded her on previous attempts. The miraculousness of the change gave Austin pause. Upon reflection, he felt it was less the result of a sudden burst of technical proficiency on her part than it was due to the new rapport between the two of them. Perhaps the knowledge of his accident had frightened her. Perhaps his kindness touched her. Maybe it was both. In either case, Kelly Wood was a changed woman, and very much a command pilot. They worked until midday, when Austin officially declared the simulator training over. Ahead of them lay another proteinaceous meal, after which she would report to the medical laboratory for final checks and the application of medical telemetry sensors. Much to her chagrin, he was getting the afternoon off.

'Don't forget,' she said as they relaxed following the meal, 'one pinch of Tetramin in the morning, and another at suppertime. Don't give too much or you'll cloud the water.'

'What do I do if something goes wrong?' he asked. 'Is there a fish doctor around here?'

'There's no such thing, at least not that I know of. Just feed them like I said, and everything will be all right. I fed them this morning, so you'll have to do the honors this evening. Think you can make it? I'm going to be occupied.'

'I'll do my best.'

'I'll try to do the same,' she said softly, reaching across the table and touching his hand.

'I wish I were coming with you,' he said, and meant it intensely.

'So do I,' she said. 'Maybe someday.'

'A few last pieces of advice. Don't sightsee until you're safely aboard Skylab. Don't look directly at the sun. You have the solar telescope array for that, and the damned thing really isn't very interesting anyway. Don't worry about things that go "bump" in the night. With all that machinery, you're going to get a few unexplained noises. It doesn't always mean the place is going to blow up. And finally, don't place all your trust in the hands of technology. Keep your eyes on the road and your hands on the wheel. Oh, and don't sneeze unless you're tied down.'

'I'll remember,' she said. 'Take care of yourself.'

'Of all the things to worry about!' he said. 'What can happen down here? Even if I get bitten by a rattler, the poor bastard would only break his teeth.'

'I'd better go,' she said, smiling.

Austin walked her to the medical lab, then consulted his watch. It was nearly 2 P.M.; the launch was scheduled for 11:57 P.M. More than five miles away, the 363-foot-tall *Athena*/Saturn assembly sat like a giant, white dinner candle, swathed in a cloud of swirling hydrogen fumes. Austin stared out of a window at it for a short time, then rode the elevator to the astronauts' quarters. He went to his room, had a brandy, and made the decision that, if an afternoon had to be killed, he could think of no better way to do it than by annoying Oscar Goldman. He freshened up, went to the parking lot, got his Mercedes, and drove to the Launch Control Center.

As Austin expected, he found Goldman hunched nervously over McCall's shoulder, peering at computer readouts which were hopelessly beyond his ability to read. Austin always felt that it was the greatest indication of

Goldman's power that he, an ingenue as far as astronautics went, was able to backseat-drive on lunar flights. Austin stole up behind him and gave him a more than necessarily hearty clap on the back. 'Oscar old pal,' he said, 'how's your instrument package today?'

Goldman coughed and composed himself, trying hard to appear nonplussed. 'It *was* fine,' he said dryly.

'In fact it's beautiful, Steve,' McCall said. 'It's the best instrument package in the world. Not a thing wrong with it. In fact, it's in such good shape that nobody need pay any attention to it until launch time, which is later this week. Steve, can you take this guy out and drown him?'

'You mean Oscar? I can't do it, Al. Too many tourists on the beach. Somebody might notice.'

'Hell,' McCall mumbled, fiddling with a knob on his console.

'I just stopped by to see if you needed me for anything,' Austin said.

'Not until we begin countdown.'

'Nine o'clock?'

'You got it.'

'Love those new, short countdowns. In the old days it was like waiting for tickets to the opera.'

'You never saw an opera in your life,' Goldman said.

'Not true. You made me go to one in Vienna once, remember? Damn near killed me.'

'I've got to get you some culture.'

'How about a raise?'

'How about an admission?' McCall asked.

'An admission of what?'

'Let's just say I have some information in which you might be interested. Those lights you saw yesterday that didn't exist . . .'

'What about them?'

'A lot of other people saw them too.'

'Where?'

'Titusville, New Smyrna Beach, and Cocoa. A couple of guys at the air-force station saw them. Two surfcasters on the beach across from Merritt Island saw them.'

'What did they see?'

'Five lights in formation.'

'Like a star. You know, like you put on top of the Christmas tree. Five points of light.'

'That's what I saw!' Austin said, excited. 'What time?'

'Same time you did.'

'Could have been meteors,' Goldman said.

'In daylight?'

'It's been known to happen. In 1974 a meteor skimmed through Earth's atmosphere in broad daylight, over the northern United States and Canada, and was witnessed by thousands of people. Photographed by dozens.'

'A million-to-one chance. And now you're going to tell me there were five of them, flying in goddamn formation?'

'Steve's right,' McCall said. 'This definitely is a little strange.'

'What do you think Steve saw?'

'Don't ask me,' McCall said. 'That's not my job. I just send mine up and bring mine back down. Don't ask me about anyone else's.'

'Anyone else's what?' Goldman asked. 'Are you seriously suggesting Steve saw something real, and that radar didn't?'

'I'm not suggesting anything. But I will tell you something, Oscar. The two guys at the AFB – both old-time fighter pilots. Now, when you got three guys with that kind of experience who make the same damn sighting, then I tend to think twice.'

'How do you know so much about this?' Austin asked.

'They call us up, what do you think? Whenever there's a UFO flap anywhere within five states, they call up to ask if it's "something weird from NASA."'

'It wasn't, was it?' Goldman asked.

'Oscar, you haven't been more than two feet from my shoulder the whole past week. I couldn't have sent up a helium balloon without your knowing it. And, Steve, I just learned some more.'

'What is it?'

'I talked to the chief of rangers at the wildlife refuge. Something strange happened there last night, a few hours after the sightings.'

'What happened?'

'A man was killed. A farmer, one of the citrus growers who lease farms within the limits of the refuge.'

'So?'

'He was killed by means unknown. All he had was burns on his hands, but he apparently dropped like a rock. He had caught a person or persons unknown attempting to steal old clothes from his back yard.'

'I'm going over there,' Austin said, heading for the door.

'Steve, don't you have to stick around here?' Goldman asked.

'I don't need him for seven hours,' McCall said. 'Would you please the man alone.' It was a moot suggestion. Austin was already out of the door and going down in the elevator.

'And while you're at it, Oscar,' McCall added pleadingly, 'would you please leave *me* alone.'

Austin drove back toward the KSC industrial area, where Route 405 provided clear and traffic-free access to and from the mainland. With a wave to the guards at the gate, Austin left the security area, crossed the long bridge to the mainland, and exited onto Route 1 northbound, the road linking the coastal towns on Florida's Atlantic shore. Seven miles along, he found that 406 was predictably traffic-choked, and continued north another sixteen or seventeen miles to Oak Hill, until he had completely skirted Indian River. Then he made a sharp right-hand turn onto Route 3, and drove south, this time on the ocean side of the river, toward the wildlife refuge. In this manner, Austin avoided nearly all the *Athena*-launch traffic, which usually came from Orlando, Disney World, and the Floridian midlands. But it was a long drive, and by the time he located the correct dirt road and followed it to Ed Hermon's farmhouse, it was nearly 4 P.M.

The small farmhouse sat amid an unnerving blaze of official vehicles, all with lights flashing. There was a Brevard County sheriff's car, two squad cars from the Titusville police, a Florida state police inspector's car, a county-morgue wagon, and a jeep belonging to the National Park Service Rangers. To Austin, the scene resembled a small Ohio town on Memorial Day. Everyone who had a red light to flash was doing so. After talking his way through a preliminary barrier of rangers and local police, Austin found a small knot of people standing around a white-draped body on an aluminum stretcher.

'Who's in charge here?' he asked.

'I am,' said a tall, swarthy man wearing the brown uniform and Smoky the Bear hat of a ranger.

'Colonel Austin, NASA,' Austin said, displaying his federal credentials.

'That wouldn't be Steve Austin, would it?' the man asked.

'It would.'

'Saw you on TV last night, Colonel.'

'Hope I didn't keep you up.'

'Nah, I was up all night with this thing, anyway. Good to meet you. My name's Bob Kemp. I'm chief of rangers here.'

They shook hands.

'Colonel Austin, this is Doc Waters ... Matt Waters, he's an MD from Titusville. Friend of mine. I asked him to have a quick look at the body. You know, the coroner takes a week to do anything.'

'Doctor, good to meet you,' Austin said.

'What can I do for you, Colonel?' Kemp asked.

'I'm curious about what happened last night.'

'What's NASA's interest in this?'

'Well, we like to keep tabs on, shall we say, odd happenings, especially in the area surrounding the Space Center.'

'I see,' Kemp said. 'Well, this sure is an odd one.'

'I understand there were some reports of a UFO last night.'

'Yeah ... our switchboard lit up all right.'

'Ours too,' Austin said in a comradely fashion.

'I don't know how many wild stories we had in here last night about funny lights glowing in the sky. You boys send anything up?'

'My boss got a little high, but that's about it.' Austin fervently hoped that the remark would find its way back to Goldman.

'Well, now we got something that isn't so funny,' Kemp said, indicating the sheet-covered body. 'Ed Hermon here, nice old guy. Grows a few oranges. He's sort of retired, you know? So last night somebody kills him. Throws acid at him.'

'Acid?' Austin asked incredulously.

'I've never seen anything like it, Colonel Austin,' Dr Waters said. 'It just burned his hands. Only his hands. It's got everyone in a tither. We don't get too many unusual criminal cases around here.'

'According to Ed's wife,' Kemp said, 'all the thief stole was some of their clothes off the line, and some fruit. And when Ed surprised him, the thief threw acid at Ed.'

'May I see the body?' Austin asked.

'You a doctor too, Colonel?' Kemp asked.

'No, but I do have a certain familiarity with medical problems.'

'I'm sure it's all right,' Dr Waters said.

Kemp shrugged and pulled the sheet from the body. The old man was still dressed in his nightclothes, his face quiet and peaceful. Austin lifted one arm and examined the hand. It was covered with a series of ugly, raised welts. Austin laid the hand back alongside the body.

'You'd better put this man in a lead container,' Austin said grimly.

'What?' Kemp asked.

'Those aren't acid burns,' Austin said, 'they're radiation burns.'

Dr Waters and Chief Kemp exchanged astonished glances.

'You sure?' Kemp asked.

'Absolutely.'

'How did it happen?' Dr Waters asked, but the only reply he received from Austin was a shrug.

'How much radiation would it take to do that?' Kemp asked.

'More than a thief could carry around without putting himself in a grave too,' Austin said.

Kemp pulled the sheet back over the body, sighed deeply, and walked away. Austin and Waters followed him. After a second, the ranger turned back to Austin.

'I think we're in more trouble than we know,' he said quietly.

'I would say so,' Austin replied.

CHAPTER FIVE

The three men stood for a long moment, each attempting to find a phrase incisive enough to use to break the silence. Finally they were rescued by a jittery young man named Jeff Lohrman, Kemp's second in command.

'The state-police roadblock has turned up something interesting, sir,' he said.

'What's that?' Kemp asked.

'The clothes.'

'What clothes?' Kemp asked, excited.

'The dead man's, sir.'

'Are they sure?'

'Yes, sir. At least, they had the initials E.H. sewed in them, and you remember when Mrs Hermon . . .'

'Said she always did that to her late husband's clothes,' Kemp finished. 'Yes, I remember.'

'The clothes were picked up tied in a bundle in the back of a Ford pickup driven by a couple from Atlanta.'

'Georgia?'

'Right. They claim they never saw the stuff before.'

'What sort of people are they?'

'Grease monkey and his girl friend. The guy is head repairman for a Ford dealership in Atlanta. The truck belongs to the shop. It's a demonstrator. They seem to be legit, sir.'

'Uh-huh,' Kemp said dully.

'What do you want to do?' the young deputy asked.

'Have the state cops hold them at the roadblock. Where is it anyway?'

'Junction of routes 3 and 402, just past our headquarters. The couple claim they were on their way to see tonight's launch.'

'Along with a couple million others,' Dr Waters said idly.

'Do these people have any sort of record?' Austin asked.

'We're checking that,' the deputy replied.

'What do you think, Colonel?' Kemp asked.

'It's a red herring,' Austin replied.

'What?'

'A false lead. A decoy. There's too many things wrong with it. First of all, do you know what auto mechanics make today? Especially ones tied up with big dealerships? That guy doesn't have to steal somebody's old clothes. Also, who drives all the way from Atlanta to see a midweek launch unless he's at least something of a man of leisure?'

'He was driving the company truck,' Kemp said hopefully.

'Tell me one thing,' Austin said. 'Was there anything else in the back of it?'

'Let's see . . . a lot of sporting equipment.'

'Like what?'

'An inflatable boat. Fishing equipment. A couple of life jackets. A cooler full of beer. A lot of beach stuff.'

'That's it,' Austin said. 'A gentleman of leisure. He is just what he says he is. A man on the way to the beach who also wants to watch the launch. He took the company pickup to carry all his crap in.'

'I'm afraid you're right,' Kemp said. 'But we have to talk to him anyway. I guess I'll go do that. Want to come along, Colonel?'

'No, thanks. I'll stay here and think awhile.'

'You really think our killer just tossed Ed Hermon's

clothes into the back of that truck?'

'It ain't out of the questiion,' Austin said. 'The way east-bound traffic is moving on 406, I'm surprised they don't have moss growing on their steel-belted radials.'

'Guess you're right,' Kemp mumbled, only to find that his mumbling was drowned by the anxious voices of others. Several rangers, clustered about their jeep's radio, were talking in quick voices and worried tones.

'What's the matter?' Kemp yelled.

Lohrman ran over to the group, took a quick consensus, then returned. 'Over by the new road leading from 406 to the spit,' he said.

'Yeah, what?'

'One of our men ... Cockrell ...'

'What, for God's sake?'

'I think he's found them.'

Kemp turned to ask Austin if he wanted to come along, only to find that the astronaut was already in his car and turning over the engine. Kemp, followed closely by his deputies, made for his vehicle and soon a caravan of official cars pursued Steve Austin's Mercedes westward down Route 406, sirens blaring and lights blazing.

'We can't just run,' Minonee said to the three other members of her family group. 'Don't be afraid. We are dangerous to them. I will talk to them. I will explain everything. This man is an official. Perhaps he will understand.'

The man to whom the Cetian referred in such optimistic terms was National Park Service Ranger Ray Cockrell, a five-year veteran of the service.

Cockrell, a bachelor, was a reasonable man, but one forced into unreasonable circumstances. Under such conditions, it is not illogical for even the most reasonable men to act impulsively, with more appreciation for the drama of the occasion than the dangers. While driving, as per instructions, along the new service road leading to the spit from which he, during his off hours, had so much success with the local population of mackerel, he stopped his jeep to inspect the interior of a large culvert. Within it, he found huddled against one wall four persons, small in stature, with shiny skin and odd, blue metallic suits. Hastening back to the jeep, he called his superior, only to receive muddled instructions which asked him both to 'hold them' and 'not touch them.' Thus confused, he drew his ·38 and went to approach the quartet.

'Don't touch them,' Cockrell mumbled. 'He's got to be kidding.'

He stumbled down the embankment and entered the culvert. Minonee rose and faced him.

'Okay, folks,' he said, 'come out of there.'

It was the first time for her. Fourteen years she had been training for that initial moment of contact. She hoped beyond hope, and spoke in English.

'We are travelers,' she said. 'We have come a long distance from another world.' Even as she spoke the words she knew that they were wrong. She felt like an ass. She knew it wouldn't work, and her suspicions were shortly confirmed.

'Yeah, sure,' Cockrell said, trying hard to sound as authoritative as the policemen he watched on television. The four fugitives in the culvert were his first arrest. He was determined to make it good. 'Where'd you get that fruit?' he asked, pointing at the few remaining oranges.

'We meant no harm,' Minonee said. 'We only . . .'

'Tell that to Ed Hermon's wife,' Cockrell snapped, waving the automatic at them. 'Get up against the wall and turn around!'

Minonee and, at her silent bidding, Eymon, turned and put their hands against the concrete. But Ilea and Keron, their parents, being aged, were slower getting to their feet and submitting to the demands of the Terran.

Angered, Cockrell pocketed his gun, grabbed Ilea and Keron by the arms, and spun them toward the wall. Suddenly he cried out and stared at his hands, palms up, as his skin turned into a field of sickening welts. Then he fell, dead, to the ground. The four Cetians stared at one another and at the inert form of the ranger. Then they turned and ran out of the culvert, back into the heart of the wildlife refuge.

Behind them, the sound of squealing tires and sirens filled the air. Austin and Kemp arrived at the culvert simultaneously, only because Austin retained from his childhood a certain reticence about defeating a policeman in any sort of competition. From his Mercedes, Austin could see the body of Ranger Cockrell lying in the culvert. He could also see the four aliens retreating across a large, grassy patch toward the woods; Kemp and several of his deputies were already hot on thir trail. But something was wrong with the scene. Austin remained in his car, which had the good fortune of occupying the best vantage point, and watched. If need be, he could always catch up later on.

The four Cetians ran in a northeasterly direction, into the middle of the forest. Kemp and his men were just behind them, yelling and running, and a large stretch of tall grass remained before they could reach the comparative shelter of the trees. In a dry wash, just out of sight of the rangers, they stopped.

'More angry men are coming,' Minonee said. 'We need your protection, Father.'

Keron looked intently at each of them. After a moment he lowered his eyes, then raised them again. When he did so, his three companions followed his gaze off to the northeast. There, as the five points of light masked the true picture of their scout ship, four images of Cetians ran out of the wash and continued toward the woods.

After a few seconds the four travelers abandoned the images which so skilfully hid their true direction of flight, and headed west, toward the Indian River.

Steve Austin rose from the seat of his Mercedes roadster in astonishment. He watched as Kemp and his men ran off toward the northeast, following four figures which were oddly unreal. Austin blinked, then blinked again, and rubbed both his eyes as one might do in symbolic removal of tiredness. But Austin was not tired, and the distress he felt was far from symbolic. Something was very wrong with what he was seeing, and he could only ascribe the difficulty to the disparity between his left eye (bionic) and his right (natural). As an experiment, Austin closed his left eye. The four fugitives appeared to be running toward the northeast, with Kemp and company in pursuit. Austin closed his right eye and opened his left. Then, the fugitives were running to the west, while Kemp and his rangers pursued nothingness toward the northeast. Austin concentrated upon the infared capability of his bionic left eye. Scanning the scene, he detected no aliens to the northeast, but found the four running figures continuing on toward the west. 'That's it,' he said to himself, 'they have created an illusion. Like a motion picture projected onto thin air. Well, let Kemp follow it.'

Austin decided to head them off. Completely alone, he drove up the service road, coming to a halt and shutting off the engine a mile on. He got out of the car and stole quietly to the side of the road. The four travelers appeared as he had predicted, crossed the narrow road, and headed into a high, hilly, rocky area bounding the Indian River. Austin took off after them, on foot, but not without escaping the notice of Minonee.

'We have deceived all of them but one,' she said breathlessly. 'Eymon . . . you must protect us from him!'

Eymon nodded and stopped running, leaving the trio to

continue on without him. He turned to face Austin.

Eymon's normally placid, even inviting face hardened into a frown as he watched Austin running toward him, a hundred yards away. He pointed at a small boulder, about two feet in diameter, then directed it at Austin. The huge rock lifted from its longtime resting place and hurled toward Austin, who was threading his way along the trail, his eyes on the ground.

Austin looked up just in time to see the projectile, and to deflect it with his bionic arm. The bolder hit his forearm halfway between the wrist and elbow, and he tossed it aside as easily as one might deflect a shuttlecock. Eymon stared at the Terran, amazed. All his training had not prepared him for a display of such strength.

And yet Austin continued tracking the four Cetians, who had, for the moment, escaped his sight. He crossed a small salt marsh by means of a broad jump so preposterously long it nearly caused him to blush. Using the infrared scanner built into his bionic eye, Austin followed a trail that was as clear as if it were written in granite. Whoever these people are, Austin thought, they are hot as hell. The Cetians' body temperature, though highly adaptable, averaged 124·7 degrees Fahrenheit. Their footsteps left thermal traces which were more than twenty degrees hotter than the temperature of the August air. Austin followed the footprints, which glowed fiery red through the mechanism of his artificial eye.

He jogged determinedly up a rock slope leading into a thickly forested area. Halfway up the slope was a wide gully across which someone had a long time before dragged a large, heavy log cut from one of the pines topping the hill. Still running at a slow but steady pace, Austin leaped onto the log, figuring on taking two quick steps to cross it. But before he could reach the ground on the far side of the gully, the log shook and flew straight up into the air, tossing

Austin onto his back on the bare ground. Austin watched with nervous fascination as the log soared high above him, then plummeted straight down toward his chest!

Instinctively Austin tucked his knees against his chest and kicked upward with both feet. He caught the log right at its balance point. The several-hundred-pound log shot back into the air and crashed to the ground fifty feet away. Austin clambered to his feet and brushed off his clothes. Further up the slope, at the edge of the pine forest, Eymon clenched his fists in frustration. Weak, nearly spent, he pointed to a foot-wide rock and sent it hurling at the Terran, only to watch Austin catch it in one hand.

Austin swept the edge of the forest with his bionic eye. There, behind a patch of scrub oak, stood a slight, thin person whose infrared reading was impossibly high. The two men stared in awe at each other for several very long seconds before Austin broke the silence.

'I suggest we stop this nonsense,' he yelled.

Frightened, unable to understand the strange Terran language, Eymon sent another small boulder flying toward Austin, who simply ducked it.

'Damn,' Austin swore, losing his temper. He cocked the arm which held the large rock he had so recently plucked from the Cetian's telekinetic beam, and threw the object at a pine tree a dozen feet to Eymon's left. The rock hit the tree with a bone-chilling crunch, knocking off chunks of bark and sending a shower of pine needles down upon the hapless traveler.

The small fit of temper over, Austin composed himself and glared at his adversary.

'Let's stop throwing rocks at each other and start acting like adults,' he called out. 'I promise I won't hurt you. I just want to talk.'

Eymon stared, uncomprehending and feeling deathly sick, then turned, stumbled, and began to run after his family. If he was going to die, he would die in their company.

'I said I wouldn't hurt you,' Austin yelled as loudly as he could, but his words were to no avail. Sighing, he started after the man.

Austin followed Eymon a short distance through the pine forest until he came to a huge tree which a recent hurricane had blown over, leaving at its base a large cavity. The cavity, gouged from the earth when the roots of the giant tree lifted up, was deep, filled with rocks and sand, and resembled a teacup set on its side. In it he saw the four travelers huddled together, shivering, staring at him in mute and wide-eyed terror. They were thin and frail in appearance, and three of them seemed sick. Even at a distance of fifteen feet Austin towered over them.

He stared at them in astonishment. They seemed to be burning up, but only three looked sick, and *all* had the same temperature. Their clothing was uniform, made of metal fabric, and, he thought, perhaps even of a metal he had never seen before. One of them could toss objects around by pointing at them and willing the action to take place. He took a step toward the group, but stopped when the young woman held up her hand.

Austin zoomed in on her hand, and his heart began to pound like a jackhammer. Her skin was shiny, as if varnished or waxed, and she had no fingerprints, no variations in skin texture at all. His mouth went dry and his brain raced. The hell with being the first bionic man. The hell with being the last man on the moon. He had just become the first man to make contact with hominoids from another planet. Shaking his head in disbelief, he stepped to one side, leaned against a small tree, folded his arms, and mumbled to himself, not at all expecting to be understood, ' "The time has come, the walrus said, to talk of many things." '

Minonee arched an eyebrow, fear suddenly replaced by

curiosity. 'What's a walrus?' she asked.

Austin pushed away from the tree and unfolded his arms. 'An aquatic animal,' he replied cautiously.

'One that lives in the ocean?' she asked.

'Yes.'

'And has the power of speech?'

'No,' Austin said, smiling, 'it doesn't.'

'Then those words you spoke ... were they poetry?'

'They were lines from an old children's story called *Through the Looking Glass*.'

'Is there more to it?' she asked, rising to her feet.

'A great deal.'

'It doesn't make any sense. It is a non sequitur.'

'It's poetry,' he said, smiling.

'We are travelers from another world,' Minonee said, using an official tone. It was a line she had rehearsed for half her life.

'I can tell that,' Austin said.

'We come from the second planet orbiting the star you call Tau Ceti.'

Austin smiled broadly and kicked at a patch of dirt.

'Is that funny?' she asked.

'Yes. You come from what our astronomers have long considered the most likely nearby place in which there might be another civilization.'

'And the same is true in reverse,' she replied. 'A hundred years ago our astronomers told us we might find something here. We did.'

'My name is Steve Austin. I'm an astronaut. I too have been into space.'

'Then ... you are from the Space Center,' she said happily.

'That's right.'

'My name is Minonee. This is my family – Eymon, my brother ...'

'We've met,' Austin said.

'And my parents, Ilea and Keron.' The three Cetians nodded at Austin and he returned the gesture.

'They will not speak to you,' she said. 'They do not know your language.'

'I think you'll do,' Austin said, taking a step toward her. 'I have a million questions.'

'Don't touch us!' she yelled.

'I understand,' Austin said. 'Just touching one of you leaves radiation burns.'

'Yes. We didn't mean to hurt anyone. But there must be something in our body chemistries which is incompatible. We are dangerous to your kind. And you are dangerous to us. The same touch that kills your people leaves a kind of illness in us. I am the only one who has not been touched. My family ... is dying.'

'Can I do anything?'

'I'm afraid not. Perhaps,' she said, her eyes suddenly dark and misty, 'perhaps we all are going to die in this strange place.'

'I'll help you ... protect you.'

'But what can you do?'

'I have some friends in high places.'

Minonee frowned. 'How are acquaintances on elevations going to assist me?'

Austin scratched his cheek. 'This is going to be harder than I thought,' he mumbled. 'What I meant is, I know people who are important in the government.'

'Oh. Your language has many subtleties.'

'You're doing very well.'

'Thank you,' she said. 'I had fourteen of your years to practice.'

'Why fourteen?'

'That's how long it took to get here.'

'My God,' Austin exclaimed, 'I could keep you busy for

years, just answering questions.'

'We are all very specialized. My task is to communicate. I am not a scientist, but I will do what I can to answer your questions.'

'Your brother is the guard?'

'Yes. He was trained to protect us. We are a unit. A family group.'

'It was your ship I saw last night, wasn't it?'

'Our scout ship. We are the first team to try to land here.'

'But I saw another one just like it almost five years ago,' he protested.

'A robot drone, sent to explore this system before we arrived. It was odd that you saw it. It only made a few orbits of your earth and moon.'

'I was on my way home from the moon at the time,' Austin said.

'Yes, of course! I remember now. I saw you walking on the moon!'

'You did? How?'

'How do you think? Television. How did you think we discovered your civilization in the first place?'

'Our radio and television emissions?'

'Naturally. For more than fifty years your broadcasts have been extending in all directions. By now, they're over fifty light-years away. That's how I learned English.'

'Incredible,' Austin said.

'Eymon tells me that you are not like others of your kind,' she said seriously.

'I'm not,' Austin said.

'He says you have great physical strength. He would like to know how that is possible.'

Slightly embarrassed, Austin cast his eyes downward.

'Look at me,' Minonee ordered.

Austin looked into her eyes, which had become penetrating and nearly hypnotic. The feeling made him uncomfortable, and he tried to look away, but his gaze was locked into hers.

'Yes,' she said softly, 'I feel the scars left by the accident. They rebuilt your body. You are more than merely human. You are partly ... how shall I say it ... mechanism.'

'The word we use is *bionic*,' Austin said, finally able to look away.

'Why did they make you so strong?'

'I ... work for my government.'

'In what manner?'

'It's hard to explain. Look. I'm afraid I'm not very comfortable with your telepathic ability.'

'I know it is disturbing to you. Why?'

'Because I have never experienced it. It makes me feel naked.'

'Unclothed? Is that considered a dishonorable state?'

'In a way,' Austin said.

'I'm afraid I shall never become accustomed to your language.'

'You'll have plenty of time,' Austin said. 'But first we have to get your family to the base hospital.'

'No. It would be no use.'

'Why not?'

'They are dying. They know it.'

'It seems to me you have all kinds of powers at your disposal. Isn't there something ...?'

'No. We lost our medicines when our ship was destroyed. It is true that we have the ability to alter objects and events, but only up to a point. They know there is nothing to be done for them. And there is nothing you can do. They would prefer to die here.'

'And you – how do you feel?'

'I am well. I was not touched by any of you. But I will die nonetheless, in a few days. I cannot live here. I need the environment familiar to me from Cetus. It is clear that I cannot live without it.'

'What happened to your ship?' Austin asked.

'I know relatively little of the technical operation of the ship. That was my parents' task. All I am certain of is that we hovered over your Space Center with the intention of establishing radio contact. But before we could do anything there was an explosion in the guidance panel. There was fire, and many circuits blew out. We crashed into a lagoon not far from our present location. We barely had time to swim ashore before automatic self-destruct decimated the ship.'

'And the ship ... it had the environment you need to survive? The one compatible with your physiology?'

'Yes.'

'Then I guess you're right,' Austin said grimly. 'I can't help you.'

'Of course, if I could return to the mother ship. But that's impossible ...'

'Mother ship? What's this?'

'Certainly you don't think we spent fourteen years in a scout ship the size of one of your trucks? The mother ship is very large, and contains a crew consisting of nearly one hundred family persons.'

'Where is it?'

'Behind the planet you call Jupiter. The mother ship is the size of a large asteroid. It could be seen by an optical telescope.'

'Can you contact it?'

'Perhaps.'

'What if I could get you to it?'

'Can you do that?'

'Maybe. But we won't know unless we try.'

Ilea and Keron stirred, helping each other to a reclining position. The older woman lay, breathing lightly, with her head on her husband's shoulder. Minonee looked at them for a long, silent time.

'It won't be long now,' she said.

'Minonee . . . I'm sorry.'

'I thank you for your tears,' she said solemnly. 'We express grief inwardly, among ourselves. Please do not be deceived if I do not respond with quite the same emotional display which I understand is common here.'

Austin stared at her wordlessly, and then at Eymon, who appeared quite suddenly to have become agitated. Being with the Cetians was an extremely unnerving experience, Austin found, because of their telepathic ability. They spoke among themselves without uttering a sound, all while showing upon their faces the most serene expressions. Austin was intrigued by the girl's reference to her family group. Apparently the Cetians were like a colonial animal, a coral. They were individual, but highly dependent upon one another and extremely specialized. They were so close that Austin wondered if the deaths of the three Cetians might not be felt back on the mother ship, if not on Cetus itself. While he thus mused, Eymon's agitation increased, and the young man struggled, with difficulty, to his feet.

'What's the matter?' Austin asked.

'There is a problem,' Minonee said, tearing her thoughts from her parents to the problem at hand.

Eymon had hopped from the group's hiding place and was walking unsteadily toward the sandy slope on which he and Austin had had their short battle.

'Where's he going?' Austin asked.

'Eymon has the power of telekinesis,' she said. 'He has the ability to move objects with the power of his mind.'

'I've noticed,' Austin said dryly.

'He is going to protect us.'

'Protect us? From what?'

'Angry men are approaching, less than half a mile away.

The men who pursued us before ... the ones my father deceived with his illusion into running in the wrong direction.'

'You father did that?'

'He also created the illusion that our scout ship consisted of five lights. And now ...'

'Look, this is important!' Austin said. 'After what has happened, my people are panicked ... angry. I'd better get your brother back here before they kill him!'

Austin stared after Eymon.

'Steve!' the girl called.

He stopped, and turned to look back at her, the sad-eyed traveler who stood, helpless, waiting for her family to die.

'What?'

'Another of the imprecise phrases you seem to love so much. Take care of yourself.'

'Count on it,' he said, and ran off, thinking that if one more person gave him that advice today, he would lose all confidence in himself.

Minonee watched Austin until his form was lost in the pine trees and scrub oak.

'What am I supposed to count, and upon what am I supposed to count it?' she wondered aloud.

CHAPTER SIX

Entirely as the result of chance, Chief Ranger Kemp had never had the opportunity to participate in that capacious form of armed conflict known as war. Had his parents but suspected his proclivities, they certainly would have planned his conception with greater consideration. But as it stood, Kemp was doomed to be too young for World War II and Korea, and too old for Vietnam. Instead, fate had cast him in the role of an aging Eagle Scout – a dispenser of poison-ivy medication and a treater of snake bites.

His reaction to the situation was to alternate resignation and fancy. During the latter moments he poured through military histories, scanned magazines dedicated to the creation of fictional Nazi atrocities, and imagined himself leading a squadron of infantry through the gloom of the Ardennes. These moments passed eventually, and Kemp shelved his daydreams in favor of the less exciting existence of a Nation Park Service Ranger. At least, he would tell himself, patting his brown shirt, it *was* a uniform, and he *had* a gun.

On that hot August day, Kemp held the gun tightly in his sweating hands as he led not a squadron of infantry but a motley mixture of rangers, state police, and concerned-local-citizens-with-shotguns up a rocky slope in the Merritt Island National Wildlife Refuge. The men were sweat-soaked, frustrated, and mad as hornets. Nothing arouses the anger of the authorities more than the death of one of their own, for each officer could see himself in the dead man who was disfigured by strange burns. The men, as they advanced upon the stand of pines that they and a team of bloodhounds had deducted was the hiding place of the aliens were vowing to have justice but praying that their prize would be revenge.

On the other hand, Steve Austin, who had seen combat that Kemp and his men could never begin to imagine, found himself driven by compassion. Running as fast as he could, which was not very fast considering the terrain, he caught up with the Cetian just as the young man stumbled to a position near where he had tried earlier to fight off Austin. There he braced himself against a tree, looking barely moments away from death.

'Eymon ...' Austin called. 'Wait!'

The Cetian looked blankly into the face of the Terran.

'Can you understand me?' Austin asked.

Eymon nodded, and Austin moved closer, holding out his hand in a gesture of comradeship.

'I know what you want to do,' Austin said. 'I understand your duty is to sacrifice yourself for your family, but maybe there's another way ...'

The Cetian turned away from Austin, but Austin jumped in front of him.

'Okay,' he said. 'I'm not going to fight with you anymore. All I can do is to try to save your sister. I am going to try to get her back to her people. I want you to believe me. If you are going to die, I want it to be with the knowledge that someone on this planet cares. Do you believe me?'

The Cetian's expression became hard, fixed, and he extended his hands, palms out, to a position where they hovered over Austin's temples. Suddenly Austin found his eyes locked into Eymon's, as they earlier had been locked into Minonee's. The exchange lasted but a few seconds, yet it left him feeling slightly drained and partially invaded. Then as suddenly as Eymon had extended his hands he withdrew them, and his expression turned to one of serenity. He smiled, then his lips moved uncertainly.

'Yes,' he whispered.

Austin returned the smile, and grasped Eymon's hand with his bionic hand. The Cetian looked at the clasped hands in horror, then realized that Austin's artificial arm would not cause the incompatibility of their physiologies to harm either of them.

'If you want to help me save your sister,' Austin said, 'keep the men off this hill as long as you can.'

Eymon nodded and whispered 'yes' once again, this time with more assuredness. Austin turned to go, but found himself still held by the Cetian. Eymon reached into a tiny, unseen fold in the waistband of his flight suit and withdrew from it a shining metal disc. This object, slightly larger than a silver dollar but with polished sides tapering to a sharp edge, he pressed into Austin's palm. Austin stared at it for a long time, then slipped it into his pocket, patted the Cetian on the shoulder, and turned back toward the center of the pine forest.

When he arrived at the encampment he found Minonee kneeling over the prostrate forms of her parents.

'They're almost gone,' she said. 'This is the end of the voyage.'

She started to cry, but ceased when her father reached out and touched her hand. Austin moved alongside and knelt with her.

'That big ship you came from – won't they be expecting a message from you?'

'Yes,' she said. 'But ... now there's no way to contact them. That was my mother's job. They'll presume we were killed, and they'll go away. They'll think your people killed us. Our civilizations will never meet.'

'Listen to me,' Austin said, 'this is important. Is there a code to use in signaling the mother ship?'

'Yes. My mother knows . . .'

'Get it from her!'

'But why? It is useless . . .'

'Minonee, it may never have occurred to you, but your mother is not the only person in the galaxy capable of using a radio. Can you get the code?'

'Leave us alone, please,' Minonee said.

Austin got to his feet and walked twenty or thirty yards away. A minute later the young woman joined him. Her face was set, hardened. 'They are gone,' she said, 'both of them.'

'I'm very sorry,' Austin said. 'But we'll have to leave them. There's no time to bury them.'

'There is no need,' she said.

Austin looked at her questioningly, then left her and walked to the depression at the base of the great tree. Where the two Cetians had been there was nothing but wisps of vapor and pieces of clothing which soon would be wisps of vapor. He returned to the girl.

'I have the transmission code,' she said.

'Take my hand.'

'But you will be injured like the others,' she protested.

'Take my hand,' he insisted.

Reluctantly she placed her hand in his. When he didn't succumb to her touch, she smiled and allowed him to lead her, at a brisk pace, through the forest.

Chief Ranger Bob Kemp led his men across the long, narrow gully which laterally bisected the slope. When he reached the ground on the uphill side of the gully he suddenly saw his quarry. Eymon was standing in plain view, next to a tall pine tree.

'There's one of 'em!' Kemp yelled. His men raised their

weapons and prepared to fire, but before a trigger could be squeezed the Cetian lifted the same log with which he failed to kill Austin and sent it rolling down the hill.

Yelling and stumbling, the men scrambled out of its path. Kemp was the first to his feet. He fired two rounds at the Cetian, both of which were lost in the depths of the pine grove. In response, Eymon fixed a hand to the tree at his right, and bent it forward. Kemp watched in horror as a sixty-foot pine shook, bent, cracked, then tumbled down upon him, its roots torn from the ground, its branches throwing from the ground a huge, swirling cloud of dust.

The men thus dismayed, Eymon turned and began to jog eastward along the edge of the pine grove, in search of another vantage point from which to rain chaos upon the Terrans without killing them. But the underbrush was thick and bullets slipped past his heels. His foot caught in a root and he stumbled forward, falling on his face. He tried to raise himself, but the strength was not his. He laid his head upon the cool green soil of the planet which had been his life's goal to reach. Staring into the sky, he died.

Less than a minute later Chief Ranger Bob Kemp, his face bearing cuts which would grow into scars that someday he would enjoy explaining to his grandchildren, walked up to where the body should have been. In its place was the form of a man, but a man who was turning swiftly into blue-tinted vapor. Kemp watched as Eymon's molecules returned to the general storehouse of the universe which spawned them. Behind him, Deputy Ranger Jeff Lohrman searched for words, and discovered nothing of importance.

'I knew we hit him,' Lohrman said.

Kemp looked at his assistant with the utmost contempt 'Shut up, Jeff,' he said. The body of the alien existed no longer. Too frightened even to shake his head in disbelief, Kemp walked off by himself.

Austin and the girl made their way quickly through the varied environments of the wildlife refuge. With gunfire echoing in the distance, they climbed into Austin's Mercedes and drove away. The service road was choked with temporarily abandoned official vehicles, and Austin had to run partially off the road in order to pass them. In a way, the fervor shown for the hunt by Kemp and his men stood Austin in good stead. Had but one of them remained behind to watch the squad cars and jeeps, Austin would not have been able to spirit off the girl.

He made his way to Route 406 and turned toward the mainland. As he did so, Minonee suddenly gasped.

'What happened?' Austin asked.

'My brother is gone,' she said.

Austin pulled the Mercedes onto the grassy strip at the side of the highway. 'I'm sorry,' he said quietly. They were silent for a long time.

'More angry men are ahead,' she said suddenly.

'More? Where?'

'About one of your miles ahead. I believe they have constructed what you call a roadblock.'

'Yes, of course,' Austin said. 'I should have thought of that.'

'What shall we do?' she asked.

'Very little. You simply will say nothing unless spoken to, and if you must talk, try to go along with everything I say.'

He slipped out of the car and withdrew from the trunk an aluminum suitcase. He laid it on the back seat of the roadster, opened it, and withdrew a black-anodized Nikon camera. He hung the camera over her shoulder, then took out a chrome-finished Pentax equipped with a 200mm telephoto lens and hung that on her as well. He snapped off the lens caps and gave her a cursory lesson in how to use the cameras.

'Look self-satisfied, confident, and even a little arrogant,' Austin said.

'Will not my appearance and clothing be somewhat unusual?' she asked.

'For Florida, yes,' Austin said, 'but you're not from Florida, you're a magazine photographer from New York. As far as New Yorkers go, your appearance is somewhat mundane.'

'Why should such a person be here?'

'To photograph the launch of *Athena One*,' Austin said.

'Of course. The first woman astronaut from your country,' she said happily. 'And you are my guide.'

'You learn fast.'

'I think I may enjoy this,' she said.

'Well, if it doesn't work, tell them who you really are. That will *convince* them you're from New York.'

Austin climbed back into the driver's seat and roared off, while Minonee occupied herself in an attempt to figure out what function was performed by the tachometer.

The eastbound traffic on Route 406 had abated somewhat as evening approached. Still, the line of cars stretched off into the distance in both directions. The traffic heading toward the mainland was minimal, and Austin lost no time cruising right up to the roadblock, which was strung across the westbound lanes of 406 smack in the middle of the bridge between Merritt Island and the mainland. The roadblock consisted of two state police cars and a pair of sawhorses. When Austin pulled up to the state trooper he already had his NASA credentials in his hand.

'Colonel Austin,' the trooper said, 'we'd been told you were in there. Do you know what's going on?'

'No. I was helping them look, but gave up when I couldn't find anything. I guess beating the bushes isn't my game.'

'We understand a trooper was killed.'

'A ranger,' Austin said.

'I hope they find whoever did it. That's a lot of woods to search.'

'Maybe the alligators got him,' Austin suggested, 'and saved us the cost of a trial.'

'Yeah,' the trooper laughed, then, using a cough as a form of grammatical transition, added, 'Colonel Austin, may I ask the name of your companion?'

'Oh, I'm sorry,' Austin exclaimed. 'This is Minonee Bruce from *Ms.* magazine in New York.'

'I see,' the trooper said. 'How do you do, ma'am?'

'Quite well, normally, thank you,' the girl said.

'Has the lady been with you the whole time, Colonel?'

'I feel like it's been forever,' Austin said, winking at the trooper, who responded to the sly insult with a smirk.

'May I go?' Austin asked. 'We have a launch, you know.'

'I get that impression,' the man said, nodding his head at the auto-choked eastbound lane. 'Go ahead, Colonel Austin. It's been good meeting you.'

Austin wagged his hand at the man, pushed the gear lever into first, and drove off.

'It worked!' Minonee exclaimed.

'Sometimes it helps, being celebrated,' Austin said.

Minonee frowned. 'What sort of celebration are you planning?' she asked.

Austin gave an agonized glance, patted her condescendingly on the knee, and continued on down the road.

Steve Austin was one of the few astronauts who had remained a bachelor. He was quite good-looking, and enjoyed the company of an assortment of women, all of whom were at least modestly attractive. Any bachelor who sees a number of attractive women is prone to obtain a greater reputation as a lady-killer than perhaps is necessary, and Austin, being a celebrity to begin with, had such a reputation. On top of it, being a bachelor gave him an abundance of free time, much of which he spent engaged in various sports, often with other Spaceport employees. Finally, he could hoist a glass with the best of them. As the result of all these factors, Austin was well-known and had many friends around the Kennedy Space Center. One of them, Jerry Kennedy, had the job of watching the main security gate.

And so it happened that Steve Austin, for only about the fiftieth time, took a woman to his quarters, an activity that was, at the very least, frowned upon. When he closed and locked the door of his one-bedroom flat atop the Manned Spacecraft Operations Building, it was after 6 P.M. The sun was in the west and, five miles to the north, the *Athena*/Saturn V stood amid a tower of hydrogen fumes.

'This is where you live?' Minonee asked, walking cautiously around the apartment.

'This is one of the places where I live.'

'You have more than one?'

'I have several. I have an apartment in Washington, I share a beach house in California, and I own a small farm in the middle of the country. The farm is my home, but I travel a lot.'

'What is the purpose of this travel?'

'I think I said . . . I work for the government.'

'In what capacity?'

'I'm an intelligence officer.'

'Ah, I see. You are a spy.'

'No, not really. I do jobs that have to be done.'

'You are a soldier,' she said, 'a warrior.'

'A soldier, no. A warrior . . . I suppose so.'

'We too had a long nationalistic phase. There were many warriors, and many wars. This phase ended two hundred years ago, when our planet adopted a federated government.

That government has existed to this day.'

'There are so many things to talk about,' Austin said.

'That poetry you spoke when we first met. Does that have a particular meaning for you?'

'Yes. My father used to read it to me when I was a child.'

'And your father . . .?'

'Dead.'

'I would like to see the rest of this poem.'

'You can punch it up on the computer,' Austin said. 'I have a fairly elaborate computer terminal here. I'll show you how to work it later on. But first . . .'

'I am hungry.'

'Oh. What do you eat? That could be a problem.'

'If you have vegetables, it will be no problem.'

'Is that what you are? A vegetarian?'

'We all are.'

'Is that the result of necessity or preference?'

'First the former, then the latter.'

'Meaning?'

'Long ago we had a thriving animal population, but we consumed many of them and killed many of the others for sport. Finally our edible species became so depleted we had had to adopt a vegetarian diet. Soon we came to like it, and now that it all we eat. Our bodies have adapted to it.'

Austin laughed slightly.

'Is that funny?' she asked.

'It is ironic. I found you in the middle of a wildlife refuge. We have much the same problem.'

'Perhaps you will solve it the same way?'

'Perhaps.'

'That is what we saw as being the principal value of interplanetary communication,' Minonee said. 'To exchange ideas, advance both civilization and humanity, and help one another avoid mistakes.'

'Is that why you came here?' Austin asked.

'Yes. For those reasons, and also for a reason which is eminently simpler.'

'What reason is that?'

'You are our neighbors,' Minonee said in a voice which was meant to indicate the obviousness of the answer. 'We came to say hello.'

CHAPTER SEVEN

Austin raided the refrigerator and fixed the girl a large salad. He joined her in consuming it, having suddenly lost his taste for meat. Then, while she explored the apartment and played with the radio and TV, he showered and slipped into a fresh suit of clothes. After that, while Austin phoned Launch Control Center to ascertain that nothing had happened which would require his presence before 9 P.M., Minonee took a shower and emerged in Austin's terrycloth robe. When she sat down on Austin's couch she was smiling slyly.

'What's so amusing?' Austin asked.

'I don't know how to say this.'

'English will do.'

'Well ... to answer the question you are ashamed to put into words ... yes, we are constructed in a fashion similar to you. Unclothed, I *do* resemble one of your women. A little less exaggerated than some whose pictures I have seen, but basically the same.'

'Minonee ...'

'Due to peculiarities in our protein structure, evolution takes place far more rapidly in us than in you. We gan gain or lose a trait in less than five generations. Consequently, we have little body hair and our digestive systems have been modified to accommodate the vegetable diet. Aside from a few organs which are in different places, our bodies are identical in basic structure. If you like, I'll take off the robe so that ...'

'No!' Austin said. 'I mean, please don't. But I would like you to do one thing for me, though.'

'What is it?'

'Stop reading my mind!'

'No. Absolutely not. It is the telepathic ability which saved our world from destroying itself. We are a very stable society, with no violence, no anticommunal conduct, and no mental illness, all because there are no secrets. We are not embarrassed by having our minds probed, because we usually do not have thoughts that embarrass us. Do you follow?'

'Unfortunately, I do.'

'I have made my morality speech,' Minonee said. 'Will you indulge me in something that now embarrasses *me*?'

'Certainly.'

'In the course of studying your culture, I found that you place a great deal of emphasis upon two things: one of them is a simple biological function which, for obvious reasons, is denied me while here; the other is a culinary matter.'

'I don't understand.'

'Steve ... will you make me a drink?'

'A drink!' he laughed.

'An alcoholic beverage,' she said stiffly.

'You're kidding.'

'*Colonel* Austin,' she said, 'I do not *kid*. On my world, humor is very vague and consists mainly of irony. As I do not know your language well enough to indulge in irony, I am *not kidding*.'

'Well, there's no reason to get testy about it,' Austin said. 'What sort of drink would you like?'

'I don't know. I've heard many names. A martini, perhaps?'

'No. Not for a start. I'll get you a glass of red wine. Don't you have intoxicants on your planet?'

'No. We can intoxicate ourselves, if it becomes necessary. It seldom does.'

'Oh, yes, the same way your brother moved things around . . .'

'We can all perform minor feats of antigravity and telekinesis,' she said.

'I'd say that some of them are more than minor.'

'That *was* my brother's training. The wine . . .'

Austin fetched and opened a botle of Chateau-neuf du Pape, and poured her a glass. She sipped it, then shrugged.

'Many years ago we had such a beverage. It was before our mental abilities were as finely tuned as they are now.'

'You are disappointed?'

'No. Hardly. It is one more indication of the degree to which our evolution is parallel. Each similarity between our races is yet another argument for the existence of other civilizations in the universe.'

'Do you want me to take the wine away?' Austin asked.

'No. Leave it. I am here, so I will live like one of you.'

'Okay,' Austin said. 'Now the time has come . . .'

'To speak of many things,' she said. 'Yes, it is time. The story really is very simple and undramatic.'

'Please, tell it,' Austin said, filling his own glass with wine and sitting beside her.

The girl shrugged. 'I had originally planned to tell it to a meeting of your most important people. At least, that was what my training prepared me for. Now, there is only you. Still, it is the same story.

'I will use your units of measurement and your language. There is no sense in confusing the issue with two sets of measuring scales and two languages. Anyway, our spoken language would be impossible for you to pronounce. Ours is a small planet, about one half the size of yours. It is the middle of three planets in our system. It lies, in relation to our sun, at a point equivalent to a spot halfway between your world and the planet you call Venus. The average temperature is well over one hundred degrees, and there are no seasons, as the imaginary line between our pole is perfectly perpendicular to the plane of our elliptic.

'As you know, Tau Ceti is, like your sun, a Class G star. But Tau Ceti has approximately one third the intrinsic brightness of your star, and a proportional size. In most ways it is identical to your sun. With one exception ...'

'What's that?'

'It emits a radiation which has made life on Cetus quite different from life here.'

'What sort of radiation?'

'You have no word for it, and we have devised no English equivalent.'

'Is it a heavy element?'

'No, it's rather a light one. You simply have no knowledge of it. There are, despite the arrogance of some of your scientists, a few things in the galaxy that you don't know about. One of them is this special radiation from our sun. It is unknown to you not because it is short-lived, but due to its low energy. It doesn't travel far. It stays within our system. But within our system its effect is profound. It has arranged our protein in such a way that evolution is greatly advanced. I think I already mentioned that.'

'You did.'

'And since our planet lies within the radiation belts of our sun, it has affected all of us.'

'It accounts for the deadly difference in our physiologies,' Austin said.

'Yes. And it also accounts for many things on Cetus. For one thing, we can never be successfully attacked. In order to visit our planet, an alien would need elaborate and sophisticated radiation shielding which would preclude large-scale invasion. That makes threat to us most improbable. As a consequence, we have no weapons technology, so you can stop worrying about the fact that we are approximately two hundred years more advanced than you.'

'Did I seem to be worrying?'

'Not exactly. You were worrying about what a man named Oscar Goldman would think when confronted with the fact of our visit.'

'You're right,' Austin said, 'that's what I was worrying about.'

'Well, we are no threat to him or you. As long as we don't touch one another.'

'Why didn't you foresee the incompalibility of our physiologies?' Austin asked.

'We did, sort of,' she said, 'but we also thought that you would shy away from us. We foresaw formal meetings across large tables where no harm could be done. We didn't think your people would be so inclined to poke, grab, and push.'

'I'm sorry.'

'What happened has happened,' the girl said. 'Anyway, due to the effect of the radiation upon our protein structure, we developed the accelerated evolution I mentioned. As a result of that, we developed the capacity to influence field forces, including gravity and electromagnetic radiation. Our radio capacity is well advanced and, of course, there is our telepathy and telekinesis.'

'That *is* how you got the bundle of clothes into the back of that truck.'

'The clothes? Yes, of course, my brother did it. Anyway, what we can do it not really so unusual. I asume you follow scientific developments on your own planet. If I'm not mistaken, it was only two or three years ago it was shown that migratory birds navigate by analyzing the planet's magnetic field.'

'Four years ago,' Austin said.

'Well, we do the same thing, only we do it a lot better. I can, with some difficulty, raise myself a foot or two off the surface of your planet. Would you like me to do it for you?'

'No. I'll take your word for it.'

'My brother could lift himself up to a hundred feet in the air.'

'I can imagine,' Austin said. 'Tell me, why didn't you employ this ability to use gravity as the basis for a propulsion system?'

'We thought of that,' she said, 'but such a system – using stars' gravity for a slingshot effect – is useful only on long voyages. On the one just completed, there are no stars in between Cetus and Terra. So what's the use?'

'What did you call this planet?'

'Terra. That was set arbitrarily by my trainers, who decided to call our planet Cetus, in accordance with your word for our star. We were just trying to standardize things. As I've said, our words are unpronounceable. So, I'm afraid that you are a Terran and I am a Cetian.'

'It's okay with me. I never cared for the idea of being called Earthling, anyway.'

'About one hundred years ago our astronomers theorized that this star system was habitable. They developed much the same arguments that your scientists have debated. The size, brightness and temperature of your star was correct. The spin period was correct. As you know, a star will spin on its axis very rapidly, unless something slows it down. Quite correctly, your astronomers concluded that the one something most likely to slow down the spin rate was planets. And once you have planets, sooner or later you have life. Since your system was about the same age as ours, there was a good chance that intelligent life ... or some kind of life ... existed here. Then, fifty years ago, we picked up the first radio signals. I think you can imagine the elation. All of a sudden, it was revealed that we were not alone in the galaxy. And not only that, but that the civilization we discovered was right in the solar system we thought it might be in.'

'There really was elation?' Austin asked.

'More than that, it was beyond a doubt the most celebrated moment in the history of our planet. Ever since we first detected your radio signals, we have prepared for the moment of contact. We set right to work on a propulsion system. We devised an ion propulsion system capable of pushing a spacecraft up to ninety-two percent of the speed of light. Incidentally, our technology bears out the theories of your Mr. Einstein. The speed of light is, apparently, an impassable barrier. I'm sorry to have to debunk so many of your science fiction stories.'

'Don't apologize to me,' Austin said, 'I don't care. Ninety-two percent of the speed of light is quite fast enough. How did you do it?'

'As I've said, my job is communication, not science. But I think it does have something to do with a peculiarly-irradiated alloy of cesium. Bombarded with photons, this alloy gives off great quantities of energy. Aside from that, all I can tell you is that it took us a month to escape our sun's gravity, and another month to accelerate to full speed. After that, we spent more than thirteen years in transmit, to travel a total distance of 11·8 light-years. In order to talk to you, Colonel Austin, I have traveled a third of my life.'

'A third? How old are you?'

'Thirty of your years.'

'You only live to forty-five?'

'That's correct. But then, forty-five of your years are equal to eighty of ours.'

'Still, you're very young-looking.'

'We age very little. You may have noticed how young-looking my parents were. They were really quite elderly.

Our adaptive abilities allow us to preserve ourselves until our ages are well-advanced. Then, when it is time, we die abruptly with no pain.'

'But if this is true, if only you have another fifteen years to live ...'

'If I started back to Cetus today, I would arrive home in time to die – is that what you're thinking?'

'Yes.'

'You're not thinking. If I spent thirty Terran years in transit at nearly the speed of light, I would age but ten years. The journey here took fourteen of your years, but on board the ship it was only five years.'

Austin frowned. 'I'm sorry,' he said, a bit embarrassed, 'but Mr. Einstein and I never hit it off. I understand the basics of relativity, but I just can't visualize them.'

'It helps to have been there,' she said matter-of-factly. 'Anyway, our mother ship contains not only many Cetians, but a library of the entire history of our planet. It contains our science, our art, our literature. Once I had made contact and the initial sensation died down, I would call the mother ship from its hiding place behind Jupiter. It would move to a parking orbit above this spot on your planet, and from there transmit down the records of the whole of our culture. Our people would shuttle down, and yours would shuttle up. Within a short time our cultures would have mingled, and both would have been immeasurably improved. Perhaps would have been participants in the formation of the first interplanetary federation in this part of the galaxy.'

'How do you know there are no others nearby?'

'We think there aren't. At least, if they do exist, they're either exactly like Cetus or they don't have radio capability. We have detected no signals from any star system other than yours. Cetus uses extremely low-power radio frequencies which are detected naturally by each of us at will. Now, the chance of such a possibility occurring elsewhere in the immediate vicinity is very small. As for the existence of a civilization which does not yet have radio capability ...'

'I know,' Austin said. 'A civilization passes very quickly, on an astronomical time scale, from no radio capability to perfect radio capability, in about one hundred years. The chance of there being a third civilization around here which is of similar sophistication to your planet and mine ...'

'Is virtually nil,' she added.

'Right.'

'And the remarkable thing,' she said, 'is that each of us suspected that the other existed. While en route from Cetus, we learned of your Project Ozma.'

'That was the listening experiment in the early 1960s?'

'Yes. Two of your radio astronomers began listening to Tau Ceti and to Epsilon Eridani for radio beacons, using the Green Belt Radio Telescope.'

'Bank. Green Bank.'

'I told you I'm not a scientist.'

'You're doing amazingly well.'

'Am I? Thank you. Well, they didn't hear anything, because we were sending out no deliberate beacon, and our regular transmissions are much too low-powered to reach out of our own system. Anyway, the attempt was most amusing. Everyone aboard the ship made quite a fuss over it.'

'It all sounds too coincidental to be true,' Austin said.

'Not really, if you think about it. Our scientists were speculating about one another, not by chance but because there really are sound, logical reasons for civilizations to have grown in our systems. After all, they grew.'

'And now they must grow together,' Austin said.

'They must,' the girl agreed, 'but they shall not unless my ship hears from me within one Terran week. Two days of it are now lost.'

'And if they don't hear, they will go home.'

'I must confess to you,' Minonee said, 'they may do that anyway. If you do succeed in putting me back on board, there will be a review by all aboard as to the advisability of contact between us at this point. The difficulties we have experienced so far will have to be taken into consideration. They may decide to wait a few decades, even a century. They may decide that panic would result on this planet. On the other hand, they may decide to bring the ship in and make contact. I am merely a reporter. The decision is not mine.'

'In any case, we have to try it. You are the first ambassador from another world. We can't let you die here. Tell me, how long would it take for the mother ship to get here?'

'Her emergency acceleration capability is considerable, especially since she's had a few days to mine Jupiter.'

'Did I hear you correctly?' he asked, astonished.

'Don't look so surprised,' she said. 'Your own astronomers have proposed it. We do it all the time. Why should one dig up a perfectly livable planet when there are others not fit for life? Your own Jupiter is a marvelous storehouse. Anyway, at full acceleration, moving into a parking orbit, twenty-seven hours.'

'Remarkable.'

Minonee finished her wine and Austin poured another glass. They discussed matters of greater and lesser importance, and Austin showed her how to live in an apartment. He gave her instructions on working the OSO General Resources Computer Readout and how to cook a meal. Without moving more than twenty feet, she could tie in to a vast encyclopedia of man's knowledge, as well as boil a potato. He showed her the television, the radio, and gave her a pair of binoculars with which to view the launch of *Athena One*. The clock flashed an electronic 8:37 P.M. Leaving her with the instruction not to open the door for anyone but him, Austin departed for Launch Control Center.

As he rode the shuttle bus north along the four-lane John F. Kennedy Parkway, which connected the industrial area with the major pads and LCC, Austin reflected on the upcoming *Athena One* launch, which was so important to NASA. The project had become, for Austin, less a priority mission than a trial of the trivial. How mundane it suddenly seemed, all the fuss over popping a small, two-person capsule in and out of orbit to test guidance mechanisms and take a few pictures of the sun. How short a distance we have really gone, he thought, and how far we have to go. There was something astonishingly silly in the specter of his rushing off to babysit a short orbital flight while the emissary from a world 68·4 million million miles away sat in his apartment, unknown to all but him, munching a salad and perhaps even watching television. How completely unreal. Then he held his bionic hand in front of his eyes and flexed his fingers, noting once again how difficult it was to tell from the real thing.

What strange days these are, he thought.

CHAPTER EIGHT

The *Athena One* spacecraft sat atop the Saturn V rocket like a pebble atop a very large firecracker. Fully fueled, the Saturn V, America's most powerful rocket in common service, contained 5·6 million pounds of propellants, with a total explosive power of 1,220,830 pounds of TNT. The Saturn V had its propellants divided into three stages.

The first and largest rose 138 feet above the launch pad and consisted of a cluster of five engines burning a mixture of kerosene and liquid hydrogen to develop 7·5 million pounds of thrust. This fuel would burn for approximately two and a half minutes. When it was expended, the first stage would fall away, and the second, containing five smaller engines burning a mixture of liquid hydrogen and liquid oxygen and standing 81·5 feet above the first stage, would fire with a thrust of one million pounds. After that, the single-engine third stage, 58·5 feet in height, would fire its LH/LOX mixture to carry the spacecraft into an Earth orbit 118 miles above the ground. Atop these three stages was a controlling computer complex developed by IBM, and atop that rode the three parts of *Athena One*.

There was the cone-shaped command module, where the astronauts rode and which would return them to earth. It was 11 feet five inches high, with a diameter at the base of 12 feet 10 inches. It contained 210 cubic feet of habitable space, including up to three astronauts, and weighed a shade under 13,000 pounds. Beneath the command module was the service module, twice as high. It carried electrical power, life support systems, and the service propulsion system which would enable Major Wood to maneuver in space. The service module weighed just over 54,000 pounds. Beneath the service module sat the orbiting astronomical telescope adapter. It sat atop the third stage of the Saturn, and was essentially a hollow tube originally designed as storage for the Lunar Excursion Module during the *Apollo* moon flights. In the Athena program the adapter was modified to contain a 24-inch Cassegrain telescope and automatic tracking mount, which Major Wood was to pluck from the adapter and attach to the Skylab structure. Its images of deep-space objects, unhindered by atmospheric disturbances, would be carried by photomultiplier and closed-circuit TV into the working area of Skylab, and beamed via telemetry from there to earthbound observatories.

The command and service modules and the telescope adapter formed *Athena One*'s hardware. It sat atop the gigantic rocket, and atop it was the 33-foot-high launch escape system, which would lift the command module safely away from the Saturn in the case of a serious malfunction during liftoff. All in all, the *Athena*/Saturn stood 363 feet high and would, upon ignition, make a noise greater than any ever made by man, with the exception of nuclear detonations.

Despite the true scientific importance of the missions, it was always that last-mentioned fact which drew the crowds to the Cape. The damned thing lit up the sky like a sun, and shook the ground until not even the most ardent skeptic could fail to be awed. By the time countdown began at 9 P.M., Playalinda Beach was packed from dunes to high-water line with bodies, binoculars, chaise longues, coolers full of beer, portable televisions and radios; in short, all the gear necessary for the comfortable viewing of an outdoor spectacle. The press area was choked with Nikons, Leicas, Hasselblads, and even an occasional American camera. A seedling forest of tripods stood with lenses aimed at the floodlighted *Athena*/Saturn vehicle. In front of a portable minicam TV outfit, local news commentator and talk-show host Jules Bergman addressed his central-Floridian audience.

'The eyes of the entire world are on this flight,' he said, or rather intoned, in that self-important broadcast manner which could make even the opening of a fish-and-chips franchise seem important, '... the flight of *Athena One*. A revived *Apollo* mission, it is designed to help discover additional sources of energy for Earth, and to help perfect automatic guidance mechanisms for orbital vehicles. The focus of attention is, of course, on the command module piloted by Major Kelly Wood, the first American woman in space. But the real surprise is the presence here of Colonel Steve Austin as flight dynamics officer ... in effect, the chief pilot on the ground. This marks the return of Colonel Austin to active duty in the space program, his first work in the line since 1972, when he was the last man to walk on the moon.

'As you probably know if you have followed the space program, the year after his moonwalk and the return of *Apollo 17* to Earth, Colonel Austin survived a devastating accident while test piloting a prototype of the Space Shuttle, which now stands on a pad less than a mile away.' Bergman paused while listening to the voice of Mission Control, boomed across the Florida beachlands over dozens of loudspeakers, then announced to his audience, 'Mission Control now advises we are one minute to launch and counting.'

The interior of Launch Control Center was a paragon of orderliness. Despite the enormity of the enterprise, the men who were at the heart of it behaved with emotion more appropriate to cutting the ribbon on a new drawbridge.

Though computers spouted figures and technicians conferred constantly to exchange numerical information, still the pace of business was extremely subdued. Indeed, most drawbridges are opened with greater emotion than is accorded the average space shot by those responsible for its success or failure.

Colonel Steve Austin, USAF, attached to NASA, sat at the end of the innermost semicircular row of control consoles. Next to him was Albert McCall, the overall project director. As Austin was responsible for the performance of the crew, so was McCall responsible for the performance of the 'hardware.' Around the two of them sat or stood an assortment of technicians, division leaders, medical personnel, and random functionaries.

As the countdown slipped under the sixty-second mark, McCall called out the names of the members of what, since the days of subterranean dugouts, has been known as the trench team:

'Guido?' McCall asked.

'Looking good to me.'

'Fido?' McCall yelled.

'Go,' Austin said from his position at the control panel.

'Retro?'

'Good here.'

'Surgeon?'

'Good,' Ruddy Wells answered.

'GNC?'

'Good.'

'INCO?'

'Good.'

'All right,' McCall said. 'We have go on all systems. CAPCOM, it's all yours.'

'Minus ten seconds and counting,' the voice of Capsule Communicator said, adding, as if the gesture were needed, 'five . . . four . . . three . . . two . . . one . . .'

'We have ignition,' Mission Control announced to all the world.

For a second nothing happened, then a sea of fire and smoke erupted beneath the rocket, and the earth seemed to quiver in its wake.

'We have liftoff,' CAPCOM announced.

'Go, Kelly,' Austin said.

'We have liftoff confirmed at exactly two minutes past the hour,' Mission Control said.

The dark, navy-blue sky turned a brilliant white, as if the sun had suddenly returned from its nightly bed or as if a supernova had without alarm turned night sky into day. The *Athena*/Saturn vehicles burned like a thermonuclear fire, sending long shadows in all directions. It shuddered and, with a great roar, lifted off pad 39A. It moved up into the night air, slowly at first, then more rapidly, until it curved off into a thin layer of cirrus clouds hanging over the ocean to the east and disappeared.

'Well, it's off,' Austin said, pushing back from his console.

'Gone but not forgotten,' McCall added.

Austin drummed his fingers impatiently on the console.

'Something the matter, Steve?' asked Goldman, who had been lurking back by the door.

'Nothing,' Austin said without enthusiasm.

'Coming up on separation,' Mission Control announced.

'We have separation.'

'Confirm second-stage burn,' McCall said.

'Confirmed,' Mission Control announced.

'Yet another hurdle passed,' Goldman said.

'Oscar,' Austin said, 'sometimes I think you never sleep.'

'Wrong.'

'Well then, you must be the only man in the world who sleeps in a Brooks Brothers suit.'

'Steve . . .'

'*With* a vest.'

'What's eating you tonight? Major Wood again?'

'She's fine. We get along just fine.'

'I know. Something you ate? You hung over?'

'Oscar, for God's sake.'

'I know what it is,' Goldman said, 'you don't like being on the ground. You want to be up there.'

'Bingo,' Austin said dryly.

'You want to return to the stars.'

'The moon will do.'

'Sorry, but I can't help you with that one. All I've got is one little Lunar Orbiter, and you're not the instrument package I had in mind for it.'

'Forget it,' Austin said, turning back to the console.

'Coming up on second-stage separation,' Mission Control announced. 'And we have separation.'

'Confirm third-stage burn,' McCall said.

'Third stage has ignited and is burning.'

'Well, gentlemen, looks like we have an orbit,' McCall said. 'Anybody for coffee?'

'I'll get it,' Austin volunteered.

'You stay put,' McCall said. 'We may need you yet.'

'What for?' Austin asked. 'It's all automatic until maneuvering and docking, which isn't for two orbits. I think I have time to make it to the commissary and back.'

'Steve,' McCall said, 'this is a multibillion-dollar installation. I think we can afford to send out for coffee and buns. We have people who run errands like that. Oscar, what are you doing?'

'Me?' Goldman said, flushed.

'Two regulars,' Austin said, smiling.

'At least it got him in a better mood,' Goldman grumbled as he walked off in search of the commissary.

The three men drank coffee and watched the mission's progress on the computer readouts spread across the large room. Operating like the efficient automated machine it was, *Athena One* achieved orbit and sailed smoothly around the globe, breaking out of Earth's shadow over Africa. The sun rose as it always does when the observer is in an orbiting vehicle – a scythe of light sweeps across the heavens, enveloping the onlooker, blotting out the stars, and turning the world from a grayish-black hulk into a field of white, blue, and green.

So many launches and so many missions had been guided through the transistors and printed circuits of Kennedy Space Center, that there occurred a slight but noticeable overconfidence. Of course, KSC had its problems and tragedies, but its successful missions far outweighed them. Though nobody acted carelessly, there was an aura of security about manned missions. People *expected* things to go right, and that expectation was borne out often enough. KSC's success record *was s*ubstantial, to say the least. Thus, when something went wrong it was always a surprise, always a shock. Thus, the failure of *Athena One* was totally unexpected and an absolute shock. It happened two thirds of the way through the first orbit, while the spacecraft was over Australia.

'This is Kennedy at fifty-two minutes,' the ubiquitous electronic voice of CAPCOM announced, 'and the station at New Zealand is about to acquire *Athena One*. We'll stand by live for this pass, *Athena*.'

'Roger, Kennedy.' Kelly Wood's voice sounded distant and static-laden. It always struck Austin as curious that the same mission technicians who kept in their living rooms two-thousand-dollar stereo systems would be content to listen to capsule communications over two-dollar speakers. 'Great day for a ride,' Major Wood said.

Austin pressed the transmit button on his mike.

'*Athena One*, this is FIDO. We promised you blue skies, Kelly, and we aim to please.'

'Thanks, FIDO. Wish you were here.'

'*Athena One*, this is CAPCOM. We would like to copy alignment results now.'

'So much for having a chat,' Austin mused to himself.

'Roger, CAPCOM. I have noun seventy-one. Check star thirty-four. Over.'

'Thank you, *Athena One*, we copy and . . .'

The voice of the capsule communications officer was interrupted by a muffled explosion, a cry of pain, and a burst of static. Instantly, all eyes in the room were wide open and alert.

'*Athena One*, this is CAPCOM, do you read?'

'Somebody clear up that channel!' McCall bellowed.

'Switching,' a voice answered.

'*Athena One*, please respond.'

'Get me visual!' McCall yelled.

'Switching to visual,' another voice answered.

A large television monitor blinked and flashed on. Through the eye of a camera placed below the instrument console in *Athena*, Major Wood could be seen through a veil of smoke, bending over Major Osterman, whose pressure suit was torn across the chest.

'*Athena One*, this is CAPCOM, what is your situation?'

Still there was no response. Major Wood was preoccupied with her copilot.

'Kelly, we heard a bang, what's going on?' Austin asked.

'It's happened, Steve,' the woman said.

'*Athena One*, what has happened?' CAPCOM asked.

'We have a problem.'

Though the beach was largely free of tourists, most of whom were busily engaged in a reverse of the day's traffic jam, and though the press photographers had abandoned their outdoors compound in favor of the comfort of the press briefing room, suddenly KSC came alive. Tourists returned to the beaches, driven by the same impulse which draws crowds to highway accidents and demolition derbies. Reporters who weren't glued to their TV monitors were harassing NASA public-relations men for information which simply was not available. Radio and TV reporters hurried into the air with a report that woke up households across the world. When NASA had 'a problem,' the situation was usually grave.

'*Athena One*, this is Kennedy,' CAPCOM announced. 'We thought we heard an explosion. Can you confirm?'

'Confirmed, Kennedy. We had a small explosion on the port side and Paul was hit by some of the fragments. He's unconscious.'

'Is there any damage to the capsule?' Austin asked.

'Can you give a damage report?' CAPCOM asked.

'We have lost the standby inboard computer. All other systems seem to be go. Internal integrity is fine, but there's no way I can scan external damage right now.'

'Can't we tell from here what blew up?' McCall yelled.

'Not without that computer,' a voice from across the room replied.

'Telemetry can't tell us anything?'

'Only what's working right. The orbit is intact.'

'Has to be a fuel line for the port reaction-control motor,' McCall said. 'Well, she's got eleven more to work with. I would say the damned thing is still maneuverable.'

'What about Osterman?' Austin asked.

'*Athena One*, this is CAPCOM. How is Paul? Where was he hit?'

'In the chest, Kennedy. It looks deep, but it's hard to tell with the suit on.'

'Take it off him,' McCall said.

'*Athena*, can you cut the suit off?'

'Affirmative. It's ripped pretty bad anyway. Wouldn't be of much use.'

'*Athena*,' CAPCOM said, 'I'm punching in Dr Wells.'

'Kelly,' Wells said, 'we've got visual on, and it looks like he was hit in the chest. Is that right?'

'That's right. He took a fragment on the left side, just below the ribs. I can't find the fragment, so I'm assuming it went deep. The cut is about four inches long.'

'Probably a piece of interior wall,' McCall mused.

'*Athena*, this is Dr Wells. I want you to give Osterman direct oxygen and one hundred milligrams of meperidine.'

'Roger, Kennedy, copy that.'

'Can you stop the bleeding?'

'Roger. I can tape some gauze over it.'

'Do we have medical telemetry?' Wells asked McCall.

'Medical telemetry?' McCall asked loudly.

'Not without the computer.'

'Can't you reroute telemetry around that computer?'

'I'll try ... it will take Major Wood. She'll have to bypass the standby computer.'

'Major Wood, did you copy that?' CAPCOM asked.

'Bypassing ...'

'We have telemetry back,' a voice announced, and a sigh of relief flooded the room.

'Get me an EKG right away,' Wells said.

'Display an EKG in front of Dr Wells,' McCall said, and a monitor near him lit up with the curious white lines of an electrocardiogram.

'Major Osterman's heartbeat is weak and fluctuating,' Wells said to McCall. 'I can control it for a while with the drugs they have on board. But we'll have to operate.'

'How soon can we bring them down?' McCall asked.

'Next orbit. We're too late for this one.'

'How long will it take to get him on the operating table?' Wells asked.

'If we operate on board the carrier, three or four hours.'

'*Athena One* to Kennedy.'

'This is Kennedy.'

'Is Dr Wells there.'

'I hear you, Kelly.'

'I took the liberty of looking inside the wound. Doctor, there is a two-inch fragment of metal penetrating the wall of the superior vena cava.'

'How far does it penetrate?'

'It's about halfway in.'

'Can you remove it?'

'Not without killing him.'

'Can *you* remove it?' McCall asked Wells.

'A surgeon could.'

'We've got to bring him down,' McCall said.

'Kennedy to *Athena One*. This is CAPCOM. Are you able to be brought down?'

'Negative, Kennedy.'

'Why is that?' CAPCOM asked.

'The only thing that's keeping Paul alive is zero gravity,' she replied. 'If we bring him back, that fragment will slice right through that vein.'

'She's right,' Wells said. 'That fragment can't be moved until a surgeon is present to seal up the wound it left. Re-entry would definitely be fatal.'

McCall stared numbly at Wells. 'What you're saying is, Osterman dies unless we send a doctor up to operate on him.'

'That's what I'm saying.'

McCall mopped his brow with an already sweat-soaked sleeve.

'My God,' he said.

'Can you do it?'

'Of course I can *do* it,' McCall exploded. 'I've sent people up often enough But it's not like riding a damned elevator. It takes time, and money.'

'How much time?' Goldman asked.

'Days! Weeks!'

'Not good enough,' Wells said.

'For chrissake, Doctor,' McCall yelled, 'what do you expect of me?'

'Humanity, Mr McCall. You can't let the world watch while America allows one of her astronauts to die in space. You have to make some sort of attempt.'

'He would be dead before we even got another rocket rolled out.'

'There's Oscar's,' Wells suggested.

'Sure, we could stick an old *Gemini* capsule on top of that one and send two people up. But tell me how we then get four down.'

'The man's got a point,' Austin said. 'There's only one way to do it.'

'What's that?'

'How long would it take to fire up the Shuttle?'

'*The Shuttle?* It's never been flown.'

'It's been flown in tests. How long?'

'Hours. All we have to do is pump in the liquid hydrogen and liquid oxygen. The main booster engines are solid propellant. They're already fired up. But . . .'

'No buts about it. We could carry a whole hospital in the Shuttle.'

'The entire thing is preposterous,' McCall said.

'It's a strange world we live in,' Austin said. 'Anyway, the idea behind the Shuttle was always to make orbital flights quick, easy, and cheap. So it gets its first operational flight a couple of months ahead of schedule.'

'I don't know.'

'It's the only idea which makes any sense,' Austin said. 'You can send up a crew including a surgeon in the Shuttle. The operation can be performed in the Shuttle.'

'It's not my decision,' McCall said.

'So get on the phone,' Austin said.

McCall sighed and thought for a very long moment. 'CAPCOM,' he said.

'Yes, sir?'

'Inform Major Wood that we are attempting to come up with a plan for rescue, and to try and keep things stable.'

McCall pushed away from his console and rose to his feet.

'Can you wake up the brass?' Austin asked.

'I have a feeling they're awake already,' McCall said, walking toward the briefing room.

'Oscar, give me a cigarette,' Austin said.

'I don't smoke,' Goldman said, 'and since when do you?'

'Since that explosion.'

'I could go for a scotch.'

'It's not on room service,' Austin said.

Goldman sat down at McCall's station at the console and patted Austin on the arm. 'I'm sure this will work out all right,' he said.

'I wish I could be sure.'

'They'll come up with authorization to use the Shuttle,' Goldman said.

'Can you help in that department?'

'Only if it were a security matter. Sorry.'

'I'm not up on politics, Oscar,' Austin said, 'but wasn't the Shuttle partially funded by the Air Force with an eye toward military space projects?'

'You're right,' Goldman said, 'it was.'

'Well then?'

'Maybe I *can* lend some weight,' Goldman said, the prospect of wielding influence having done much to improve his outlook. He excused himself and hurried after McCall, not wishing to miss a moment of that man's meeting with the upper echelons of NASA administration. It was nearly one-thirty in the morning. Austin buried his face in his hands and leaned forward against the console.

After a few moments Rudy Wells, who had been off conferring with technicians and other doctors, returned. 'Where's Oscar?' he asked.

Austin raised his head from the console. 'Off showing the NASA brass what power means,' he said.

An hour and a half later, a beaming Oscar Goldman returned to the firing room, followed closely by Albert McCall and a posse of NASA officials. McCall sat at his station. 'CAPCOM?' he yelled.

'Yes?'

'Get me the capsule.'

Kennedy to *Athena One*, do you read?'

'This is *Athena*.'

'Stand by for the project director.'

'Kelly, this is Al McCall. We have decided to send up a surgeon in the Shuttle. It will take six to eight hours to accomplish liftoff. Do you copy?'

'Roger.'

'Do you think Paul will last that long?'

'Yes, I think he will. As long as he stays in zero grav and we don't get knocked around.'

'Is the bleeding contained?'

'No problem. His condition is stable and looks like it will remain that way for a while.'

'You will rendezvous with Skylab as planned. The operation will take place either in Skylab or in the Shuttle, as the surgeon sees fit when he arrives.'

'Kennedy, may I ask the name of the surgeon?'

'We don't know yet, *Athena*. As you know, we have no surgeon with astronaut training.'

'May I ask if you have selected the Shuttle pilot yet?'

'We have made our selection, *Athena*. The rescue mission will be commanded by Colonel Austin.'

'Good,' the woman answered.

Austin froze. His face turned pale, and he thought that if he touched his finger to his cheek it would feel like a block of ice. For the first time in as long as he could remember, he couldn't think of a thing to say. Aghast, he looked at Oscar Goldman, whose features had about them the inner glow of the completely self-satisfied.

'Is Steve there?' Kelly radioed.

'Affirmative, *Athena*, but I don't think he's in any condition to talk.'

Kelly laughed. 'When he recovers his composure ask him to give me a buzz.'

'Will do, *Athena*. Prepare for switchover to CAPCOM for receipt of rendezvous instructions.'

McCall flipped a few switches, then left it to the firing-room technicians to arrange the necessary maneuvers. 'Steve,' McCall said, 'I'll need you, Oscar, and Rudy down the hall in briefing-room A.'

'Al . . .' Austin stammered.

'*Now*, Colonel,' McCall said, leading the way. The briefing room was quite ordinary and might have been found in any of a thousand company headquarters. It contained a long, imitation-wood table surrounded by black vinyl chairs, a green blackboard, a large TV monitor, a computer readout panel, and a retractable movie screen.

'Coffee, gentlemen?' McCall asked.

'No,' Austin said.

'Come on, Steve, you're not going to get much sleep for the next couple of days.'

'Al, you know I'm not qualified . . .'

'Wrong! You are qualified to fly the Shuttle. If you mean to say there are pilots with more simulator experience than you, you're right. But considering the range of your abilities, you're the only man for the job.'

'What range? What are you talking about?' Austin asked, looking warily at Oscar Goldman.

'I told him, Steve,' Goldman said. 'He knows you're bionic.'

'Oh,' Austin said.

'You see,' McCall continued, 'there's another cat to be let out of the bag.'

'And what is that?'

'The explosion aboard *Athena* did more than wound Paul Osterman and blow out the standby inboard computer. It tore up the release mechanism for the docking hatch. When Kelly docks with the Shuttle, she's not going to be able to open the hatch. Of course, she could still suit up and blow the hatch using the explosive bolts, but that would kill Paul. No, you're going to have to force it from inside the Shuttle. Then you take Osterman into the Shuttle, where Rudy will operate.'

'Who?' Wells said.

'You,' McCall said.

'This is quite a day for surprises,' Goldman said.

'More than you know,' Austin commented.

'You've flown in Air Force jets,' McCall said to Wells. 'That's close enough. Anyway, the Shuttle is designed to act as a ferry. One of its jobs will be to take scientists to and from orbiting laboratories. You're certainly more physically fit than most astronomers. I mean, you ain't as young or good-looking as Carl Sagan, but you'll do.'

'I always did sort of want to,' Wells admitted.

'See? And this is your only chance, Rudy. If we had more than a couple of hours, we would get some hotshot young Air Force surgeon. This is your last chance to get into space.'

'And look at it this way,' Goldman said, 'think of the publicity. Can you imagine what you'll be able to charge for an appendectomy?'

'Ever practical,' Austin commented.

'Isn't he,' McCall said.

'Tell me one thing,' Austin said. 'Why are you having Kelly rendezvous with Skylab?'

'You're going to be up there three or four days, until Osterman's well enough to be brought down. You might as well use the time to assemble the orbiting astronomical telescope and tie it in to Skylab's telemetry. That way, we can salvage some of the mission.'

'Fine,' Austin said.

'Then it's settled. The Shuttle crew will be at work by now. Liftoff is tentative for 9 A.M. Steve, you and Rudy suit up and get over to the Shuttle simulator. You'll meet the copilot there.'

'Who's that?' Austin asked.

'Ed McCarthy.'

'No problem.'

'I have a problem,' Wells said. 'This is all very exciting, but we all must face the facts of the case. So what if Major Wood is a nurse. So what if I'm a good doctor. The fact is, we've got one chance in ten of saving Osterman. At best, one in five. The kind of operation he needs normally takes *weeks* of recovery, not days. And when the weeks are up, maybe you let the man sit up in bed, not endure the stresses of re-entry. The fact is, no matter how good I patch him up, he will probably die before splashdown.'

McCall sat in thoughtful silence for a moment.

'I just don't think I can save him,' Wells said.

'I can,' a voice said. The four men quickly turned toward the door. Leaning against it was a woman dressed in a bluish woven-metal flight suit, her arms folded as she once had seen Austin do.

'Minonee,' Austin gasped.

CHAPTER NINE

McCall, Wells, and Goldman walked, wide-eyed, toward the girl.

'Don't touch her,' Austin cautioned, 'she's radio-active.'

The three men stopped, uncertain.

'You'll be safe if you stay across the room,' Austin said.

'Actually,' the girl corrected, 'four inches is quite far enough.'

Austin walked to her. 'Why did you come here?' he asked. 'I told you to stay in my apartment.'

'I think I answered that question,' she said.

'You mean, to save ...'

'Your astronaut. That is correct.'

'But how ... yes, of course,' Austin said, waggling his index finger to indicate the Cetian ability to manipulate objects.

'Not me personally,' she said, 'but to borrow your phrase, I too have friends in high places.'

'Of course ... your mother ship.'

'Our surgeons can deal with the matter quite readily. We can't make him better than new, as Dr Wells did with you, but we certainly can make the man capable of withstanding re-entry. And, I might add, it would also solve the problem of what to do with me.'

'A rendezvous in orbit between the Shuttle and your ship?'

'Precisely.'

'Steve,' McCall broke in, 'who is this woman?'

Austin sighed. 'Gentlemen,' he said, 'I'm only going to say this once, so please listen carefully. And since we are involved in a serious situation, I think you can try to believe that I'm not wasting your time with games. This woman's name is Minonee. She is an emissary from the second planet circling the star we call Tau Ceti. Her scout ship was the UFO I saw yesterday. She tried to make contact with us, but there was an explosion and the ship crashed into the river and was destroyed.'

Rudy Wells circled the woman, peering at her hair and skin.

'Your skin has no lines, no markings. It is perfectly smooth,' he said.

'That's right.'

'What is the nature of the shiny quality?'

'A protective secretion,' she said. 'It is a compound with some similarities to the compound you call polyvinyl chloride.'

'When did you try to make contact?' McCall asked.

'Shortly after two in the afternoon.'

McCall stiffened. 'At two-ten yesterday afternoon,' he said, 'a female voice broke into our capsule communications and spoke three words before the broadcast broke up in static.'

'The words were "request permission to,"' she said. 'They were the first part of the sentence "Request permission to speak on this frequency on a matter of extreme importance."'

'She's right,' McCall said, throwing up his arms.

'Why didn't you mention that before?' Austin asked.

'It didn't seem important. We thought it was some kid with a ham radio.'

'Incredible,' Wells said, 'absolutely incredible. I wish I

could touch your skin.'

'You can't. Three of us and two of you have already succumbed to our touch. It seems that our physiologies are so radically different, that a touch is fatal to us both; to you, from radiation burns; to us, from some kind of tissue breakdown.'

'How did you get in here?' McCall asked. 'There are any number of security guards.'

'Please don't blame your subordinates,' she said, 'I ... influenced them. They are not to blame.'

'She can be very persuasive,' Austin said.

'No!' McCall exploded. 'This is too much! I won't hear it. This is the biggest load of ...'

'Mr. McCall,' Minonee interrupted.

'What?' he screamed.

'Look into my eyes.'

McCall glared at her, the frustrations and agonies of the day turning to fury with the appearance of this newest surprise. But once his eyes were locked into hers, he found that he couldn't remove them. He tried twisting his head, but it wouldn't turn. He tried shielding his eyes, but his arms were like lead, and hung heavily by his sides. Minonee extended her hands near McCall's temples. When she withdrew them and broke eye contact, McCall stumbled backward into a seat.

'I'm sorry, Ambassador,' he said, 'but I seem to have forgotten what I was saying.'

Goldman and Wells stared at him in awe.

'Ambassador?' Austin asked.

'That *is* my title.'

'Yes,' McCall said, 'it is.'

'Steve, do you have a cigarette?' Goldman asked.

'You don't smoke, Oscar.'

'I do now.'

Austin laughed. 'Rudy, give the man a smoke. If he rots

his lungs out, you can always make him new ones.'

Wells reached into his jacket pocket and withdrew a package of Kools.

'Are those cigarettes?' Minonee asked.

'Unh . . . yes,' Wells said.

'May I see them?'

'Sure.'

He walked cautiously to her and dropped the package into her palm.

She held it in front of her and frowned at the package. Then, with great concentration, she caused the pack to rise a foot into the air, and travel half a dozen feet to a position in front of Goldman, who stared at it in horror, afraid to touch it.

'Please take the cigarettes, Mr. Goldman,' she said. 'I cannot do this forever.'

Cautiously Goldman plucked the pack out of mid-air.

Minonee let out a sigh, glad that the effort was over.

'You never told me you could do that,' Austin said.

'I said we can all perform minor feats of telekinesis and gravity control. I also said I wasn't any good at it. That little parlor trick, to use two more of your pet phrases, damned near killed me.'

'Parlor trick?' Goldman asked.

'You should have met her brother,' Austin said.

'I always knew there was somebody out there,' McCall said. 'And you know what? I always knew one day they would show up, just sort of drop in for a chat. But I never expected to see it. Tell me, why did you come *here*?'

'What place on this planet is more logical?'

'Of course.'

'And when we crashed, Steve rescued us. He saved my life. Now I wish to repay him. I can save your Mr Osterman. Let me call in my ship. They will arrive in about twenty-seven hours. I will go on the Shuttle with you. Our surgeons will have no trouble with his injury. After all is well, I will rejoin my ship.'

'And then?' Austin asked.

'I will report on what happened, and we will see what ensues.'

'I don't understand,' Goldman said. 'What *might* ensue?'

'Either my people decide to establish ties with your people, or we go home. Either we agree to put our ship in orbit and arrange for an exchange of cultures, or we don't. Mr Goldman, I know you are a military man ...'

'Intelligence.'

'Whatever. You are worried about the fact that we are two centuries more technologically advanced than you.'

'It had occurred to me.'

'As I told Colonel Austin, because of the nature of the radiation belts surrounding our star, we cannot be successfully attacked. Therefore, we have no weapons technology. Our defensive abilities are limited to what we can do by way of telekinesis and gravity control. And not all of us can do much with that. Be assured that we are no match for you in a fight.'

'I wasn't really worrying ...'

'Yes, you were,' she corrected. 'And one more thing which concerns you – our technology would be of little military use to you, as so much of it is dependent entirely upon our physical presence. Certainly, we could teach you a great deal of a scientific nature, and you could teach us much. For example, our agriculture scientists are most eager to learn your crop-production techniques. Things don't seen to grow as well on Cetus as they do here. And Mr McCall would, no doubt, be interested in our ion drive.'

'I see,' Goldman said. 'Then, the stakes are ...'

'The stakes are, either my people feel you are ready for an exchange or they don't.'

'Ready? What do you mean, ready?'

'Certainly *you* are ready, Mr Goldman, as are your scientists. But there does seem to be a difference between you and the general population. Those men who pursued us with guns, for example.'

'They were frightened and angry,' Austin said. 'They thought you were common murderers.'

'But I *told* that policeman who we were and bade him not to touch us.'

'You didn't expect him to believe you?'

'Of course. If you landed on Cetus quite unexpectedly and said who you were, even the most ordinary citizen would at least give you a hearing.'

'Perhaps we *are* too different,' Austin mused.

'Steve,' Goldman said, 'I would appreciate your being less negative. Miss ...'

'Minonee.'

'Minonee, we simply *must* make this work. There is so much to teach one another.'

'That is my feeling as well. However, I am not the one to decide. There are a hundred of my fellow Cetians in a large ship, out beyond the orbit of Jupiter.'

'They're *mining* Jupiter,' Austin said, with deliberate seriousness.

'Mary mother of God,' McCall swore.

'I beg your pardon?' the girl said.

'A colloquialism,' Austin replied.

'Steve, while you were away, I figured out that approximately forty percent of your language is either unnecessary, meaningless, or both. A great deal of it means nothing at all. See. You've even got me doing it. I said, "nothing at all." The "at all" was redundant.'

'There are more important things to worry about,' Austin said.

'I just found it amusing.'

'Right now we have to get going on the rescue. The hours

between now and then will provide ample opportunity for us to exchange information. I already know enough, Oscar, to keep your scientists busy for a decade.'

'Can you teach me how to do that trick with the cigarettes,' Goldman asked.

'No, I'm afraid not. You have to be born with it. Like I told Steve, it's an extreme evolutionary adaptation of the same ability by which your migratory birds navigate. They detect field forces. We can employ them. Aside from that, not even our best minds know exactly how it's done.'

'Wouldn't that be something, Steve,' Goldman said, excited. 'With that ability, I could cause ulcers all over the Soviet Union.'

'I'm afraid you won't have the opportunity,' Minonee said dryly.

'We really have to get going on the rescue,' Austin said.

'So it's settled,' McCall said. 'The Shuttle carries ten people. One more won't make any difference. Now, I'd like to hold down the number of people who know about Minonee. There are the four of us. I'll need to tell the firing team, plus five men in the ground crew. She'll need a pressure suit, and that adds a few more. I think I can get away with telling twenty people. That's not too bad. They are all completely trustworthy.'

'We'll have to sneak her past the press,' Austin said. 'It might be a little awkward if they knew we're bringing back down one less person than we're sending up.'

'That *would* tend to intrigue them,' Goldman said.

'Is there anything you need?' McCall asked.

'Yes,' the girl said, reaching into a fold in her clothing and withdrawing several sheets of NASA stationery on which she had made notes.

'Can you scan and transmit visual information out as far as Jupiter?' she asked.

'No problem,' McCall said.

'Good. You'll have to transmit the data on these three sheets. The frequency is noted in the upper left-hand corner. Please transmit the data in this order, and repeat it three times. Oh, and at the end of it please add a blueprint of the docking adapter for your Shuttle.'

'What's in that data?' McCall asked.

'A situation report and a request for assistance.'

'And you're sure they'll come?'

'They'll have to. We are a very communal people. The death of one of us touches us all. They could no sooner abandon me than they could their own family groups.'

'And you said it would take them how long to get here?' McCall asked.

'Approximately twenty-seven hours,' she said.

'My God. That sounds so impossible.'

'So does finding two civilizations at approximately the same stage of development living just 11·8 lightyears apart,' she said. 'But nonetheless it is true.'

'I would love to take a look at your propulsion system.'

'Perhaps it will be possible. Perhaps also we can learn of your agriculture.'

'This could be a great day for both our cultures,' Goldman said.

'If it is better than yesterday,' she said, 'I will be satisfied.'

McCall walked to the door and opened it. 'I'll select the team and call them in here,' he said. 'Steve, you and Minonee stay put. I'm afraid we're going to have to put her through a whole new series of introductions.'

McCall departed, followed shortly by Oscar Goldman.

'Where are you going?' Austin asked. 'I thought you had a lot of questions about Cetian technology.'

'Oh, I do,' he said. 'I'm going to pick up a cassette recorder. And I'm going to try my hardest to find something for her.'

'What's that?'

'What else? A farmer,' Goldman said, closing the door behind him.

At 3:15 A.M. the floodlights were turned off at pad 39A, from whence the *Athena*/Saturn had lifted off, and were turned on at 39B, where the giant Space Shuttle sat. The Shuttle, painted in the red, white, and blue typical of American space vehicles, came in four parts. The orbiter, a delta-wing aircraft measuring 120 feet in length, carried a liquid oxygen/liquid hydrogen engine. The orbiter stood vertically on the pad, nose up, its belly resting against a large, external LH/LOX fuel tank which itself was flanked by two solid-propellant boosters. During liftoff, all engines would be fired, developing a total thrust of 6,141,000 pounds. The Shuttle would lift off vertically, then arc off to the east. Twenty-five miles high and about six hundred miles downrange, the two solid-propellant boosters would be jettisoned and would fall into the sea. Recovery vessels would then retrieve the boosters and return them to KSC for refurbishing and re-use. Just before orbital insertion, when the Shuttle reached a velocity of approximately seventeen thousand miles per hour, the expendible, exterior fuel tank would be jettisoned. When the orbiter completed its mission, retro rockets would brake it to re-entry speed, then it would fly through the atmosphere to a normal aircraft landing on the KSC Shuttle strip.

The lighting of 39B brought new life to the corps of press photographers and television crews, who were forced for the second time that night to shift location. With élan of an intensity approaching panic, they rushed from the comfort of the press room back out to the press grandstand area, which was within the confines of pad 39 but still three and a half miles from the Shuttle. By 4 A.M., scarcely forty-five minutes after the Shuttle was illuminated, news programs around the world were broadcasting the word that NASA was sending up the long-in-planning Space Shuttle to rescue its stricken *Athena* capsule.

At four-ten, the newsmen's deductions were made official by the release of a simple, two-page statement:

> Shortly after achieving orbit, *Athena One* suffered an explosion in one of its twelve maneuvering jets. The explosion caused the loss of the standby inboard computer and damaged the docking hatch. The integrity of the capsule remained unaffected, and it is still operational. However, copilot Osterman was seriously wounded by a piece of flying metal, which is lodged near his heart. Since immediate re-entry is not possible without gravely endangering Astronaut Osterman's life, the National Aeronautics and Space Administration has decided upon a rescue mission. Therefore, at a yet-to-be-decided time, a surgeon and a team of astronauts will be fired into orbit in the Space Shuttle, which will be pressed into service six months in advance of its first scheduled flight. The surgeon is Rudolph Wells, MD, who is flight surgeon on the *Athena One* mission. Copilot is Lt Edward D. McCarthy; mission commander and pilot is Col. Steve Austin. Dr Wells will assess the situation and, if necessary, operate on Major Osterman, using an operating facility being constructed in the Shuttle. Further details upon receipt.

Re-usability and economy were not the only advantages of the Shuttle. Another was size. It was, compared to such average manned capsules as *Apollo* and *Athena*, absolutely huge. Behind the four-seat crew-and-passenger area was a payload bay measuring sixty feet by fifteen feet, capable of carrying sixty-five thousand pounds of cargo. As soon as the ground crew was given the go-ahead, this cargo area was turned into the astronautical equivalent of a field hospital. In it was positioned an assortment of OR equipment borrowed from the Cape Kennedy Air Force Station. The appropriate electronic diagnostic and therapeutic devices were centered around an operating table and connected the Shuttle's electrical system. All devices were bolted to the floor, which was at that moment the wall, due to the vertical launch.

At five-fifteen a red, white, and blue mobile home, used to convey the astronauts from the suiting-up area to the pads, rolled along the five-mile length of Kennedy Parkway and up the access road to pad 39B. As it pulled to a halt in front of the launch-tower elevator, which had been cleared of all but a few select crewmen, the floodlights suddenly faltered and blinked out. In the press compound, where dozens of long-range telephotos were trained at the site, pandemonium reigned while distraught NASA public-relations men attempted to explain away the 'temporary electrical failure.' The electrical failure lasted fewer than ten minutes. Before it was over, Austin, McCarthy, Wells, and the girl were being assisted, unseen, into the cockpit of the Shuttle.

The Shuttle cockpit, unlike the previous manned capsules, was shaped like that of a commercial airliner. Hence, it had a forward-looking window, so, for the first time, an astronaut would be able to see clearly where he was going upon liftoff. Surrounding that window was the expected instrument array, and behind it, two rows of paired, reclining seats designed to absorb the force of acceleration without greatly inhibiting movement. Behind those four seats, technicians hastily installed two others, one of which was a special sort designed by a NASA engineer, during an idle moment, with an eye toward space rescues that nobody ever seriously anticipated would occur. It sat on a cicular track and thus could revolve through 360 degrees so that an injured man who was supine in space would not find himself in an erect posture upon landing.

The crew was strapped in by 6 A.M. and plugged into telemetry and waste-elimination systems by seven. At seven-thirty the countdown began, with liftoff set for ten. Just after the initiation of countdown, McCall paid a final visit to the girl, followed by Goldman, who had been absent most of the night.

'Oscar, where have you been?' Austin asked, staring at Goldman from a rather awkward position which made the OSO chief appear upside down.

'Out collecting,' Goldman said.

'Collecting what?' the girl asked.

'Miss . . .'

'Minonee,' she said.

'Whatever,' Goldman replied. 'The crew is strapping down three gray-leather suitcases. They are a present from me to you.'

'Indeed.'

'Do you know what microfilm is?'

'I presume it is a miniaturized information system.'

'That's right. Microfilm contains information that has been reduced on photographic film. Your people will have no trouble devising a machine with which to read it.'

'What have you given me?' she asked.

'Microfilm records. One suitcase includes microfilm of The *Encylopedia Britannica.* The other two suitcases include microfilm of the past fifty years of *The Journal of Agricultural Science.*'

Minonee's face became quite brilliant. 'Thank you,' she said, 'it means so much to us.'

'Included also is a plastic package which contains five compartments. In three of them are seeds of especially productive strains of wheat. In one, barley. In the third, soy.'

'Thank you, Mr Goldman,' she said. 'Colonel Austin has the tape recording we made detailing basic information about Cetus. When we rendezvous with my ship, I will endeavour to . . . how do you say it . . . talk them out of . . . a description of our ion-propulsion system.'

'That will make Al McCall very happy,' Goldman said.

'Unfortunately for your purposes, Mr Goldman, the system is of no use in journeys of fewer than one or two astronomical units. Unless you are going more than one or two times the distance between your planet and its sun, it will do you no good. So, for your military purposes . . .'

'Miss Ambassador,' Goldman said haughtily, 'it may never have occurred to you, and I'm sure that Colonel Austin never saw fit to mention it, but I *am* a human being. I do contain at least a spark of humanity. I do occasionally find myself interested in matters which have absolutely nothing to do with national security.'

'That is good,' she said. 'That is the first step.'

'Whether it is or whether it isn't,' he said, 'that is the case. And let me tell you one more thing. It is my intention to share the knowledge of your arrival with Russian intelligence. Or rather, NASA will share it with those in the Russian space program. As you have so aptly pointed out, you are of no military importance to us, so it does not in any way behove us to keep your visit secret from the Russians. They will know that something is afoot anyway. They are not as easily fooled as our press corps.'

'Will you tell the general population?'

'No.'

'Why not?'

'They would not believe us. And not only would they not believe us, they would think we aren't playing with a full deck.'

'Excuse me?'

'They'd think we're crazy,' Austin said.

'Oh. I see. And then they would reduce your budget,' she said, smiling.

'You learn quickly,' Goldman said.

'Cynicism is contagious in this place,' she commented.

'Well, I have to go,' Goldman continued. 'There is only one more thing. Steve asked me to give you this.' Goldman handed the girl a book, wrapped in blue paper.

'What is it?'

'A copy of *Through the Looking Glass*,' Goldman said, adding, 'God knows why he wants you to have it.'

'God may not know,' she said, 'but I do. Once again I thank you.'

Goldman departed, and two tower technicians shut and locked the crew-access hatch. For the next hour and a half, pilot Steve Austin and copilot Ed McCarthy were on the radio with CAPCOM, checking various channels, circuits, and instruments. At 9 A.M., with the sun just beginning to warm the acres of foliage and exotic animals at the wildlife refuge, visible to Austin on the port side, the final countdown began. Precisely at 10 A.M. the Shuttle would lift off, carrying its most unusual cargo.

Austin eased his microphone away from his lips and twisted in his seat so that he could see Minonee, who was in the second row of gravity seats. Behind them, the payload area of the Shuttle swept back a seemingly endless distance. Within a few years, that space would contain for transportation into space the building materials for a permanent space station, where men and women could work with ease and in comfort. Then, Austin thought, man would truly have grown his space wings.

The Shuttle was the real beginning. All the earlier manned flights were preludes, risky and temperamental. Austin surveyed the interior of the craft, all burnished black, vinyl, and electrical, and though it resembled more than anything the cockpit of the Concorde Supersonic Transport, which he had seen during a mission in France. Within it, both Rudy Wells and the girl seemed rather pensive.

'Rudy?' Austin asked.

'Nothing,' Wells said uncertainly.

'What's the matter? Come on, Doctor, you can tell me.'

'Can I?'

'Not a word to Oscar. I promise.'

'I don't know how to say this,' Wells said.

'You're scared . . . right?'

'Right.'

'And that makes you feel bad?'

'Of course it does.'

'Why shouldn't you be scared, Rudy? Think about it. Space travel is now in roughly the same stage of development that atmospheric flight was right after Lindbergh. It's safer than airplanes were in 1928, but it's no more common. You're correct to be scared. Three very powerful engines are about to hurl you right off the face of the earth. But if you study the odds – NASA's success/failure rate – you'll end up worrying about something more normal for you, like the end of the trout season.'

'Don't you worry, Steve?'

'Not anymore. As the saying goes, I have met the enemy and he is mine. I've been there before; the entire thing is automated to the nth degree. This ain't some New York-to-Chicago shuttle which costs maybe ten thousand bucks to put in the air. Our employers are dropping ten million on this little flight. You don't for a moment think they would do that if the odds were other than impressive.'

'I guess you're right.'

'Of course I am. I wish you would stop thinking of me as a Tinker Toy and begin regarding me as an adult human being with emotion and intelligence.'

'Steve . . .'

'Don't apologize, Rudy.'

'Tell me . . . what does it feel like?'

'What does what feel like?'

'Liftoff.'

'Oh, that. It's overrated. It feels like you're in a movie theater and some fat lady falls on you. Nothing more dramatic than that. The adrenaline more than overcomes it. On my first orbital flight I was so excited I didn't notice the G-forces. Rudy, just sightsee and let Ed and me worry about flying the thing. The only thing you've got to do is keep your visor down during liftoff. Things will be okay for the first half minute, but after that we'll be staring directly into the sun.'

'I understand.'

Austin turned his attention to the girl. 'How are you?' he asked.

'Not bad.'

'You know what bothers me about you people,' Austin said, smiling. 'You always define how well something is by stating how bad it isn't.'

The girl's cheeks turned red.

'You're blushing!' Austin said. 'You're really blushing!'

'I don't know why I need be embarrassed by your language,' she said.

'But you are.'

'Indeed,' she said. 'If I don't get home soon, I think I'll go bananas.'

She laughed at the inquisitive frown on Austin's face. 'That was a joke,' she said. 'Wasn't it funny?'

'Better than some I've heard,' he said.

'See! You're doing it yourself! You said it wasn't bad. You didn't say it was good.'

'It wasn't,' Austin said dryly.

'Then why didn't you say that in the first place?' she asked. 'You talk so illogically.'

'My dear woman, the language has been in use for a

thousand years. You can't expect that in all that time somebody didn't inject a few red herrings.'

'Why should anyone want to put fish in his speech pattern?' she asked.

'Oh, never mind,' Austin said. 'Look, the sun is breaking over the wildlife refuge. To the left.'

'I see,' she said, craning her neck to see out the windscreen.

'What sort of animal life is there on Cetus?' he asked.

'Similar to your tropical animals. As I said, we have no seasons, but the average temperature is quite warm, at least near the equator. However, there is a difference. The tropical animals are predominantly small and consist mainly of birds. The polar animals are larger and mammalian. There's nothing as dramatic as some of your animals. They don't seem to grow as large, and they certainly are a *lot* quieter.'

'You probably just ran into a couple of old 'gators,' Austin said. 'Scared me half to death the first time I heard them, too.'

'I did see a turtle,' she said. 'We have several species like that.'

'Where on the planet do you live?'

'There are two large continents located equatorially, and several minor ones in the cooler zones. I live on the largest of the two equatorial continents.'

'Which is why your body temperatures are so high.'

'Correct. Of course, it does cool somewhat as one moves further from the equator, and there are small polar ice caps. Sometimes we go toward the polar regions for a change.'

'Did you live with your family?'

'You mean, in the same home?'

'Yes.'

'No, of course not. I live alone, more or less. Much the same as you, I imagine.'

'Do you have a lover?'

'Yes. He is the chief engineer on *Cetus One*.'

'*Cetus One?*'

'What we have been referring to rather loosely as the mother ship.'

'Oh. That implies there may be a *Cetus Two*.'

'It is under construction. Just in case we go ahead with the cultural interchange.'

'What is your lover's name?'

'Etan.'

'Why don't you live with him? Do Cetians marry?'

'Not in the sense that you do. We take mates, but it is by your standards rather a complicated process.'

'It can get fairly involved here.'

'Cetians are extremely communal, as I said. Our entire society is built upon family groups. In order for a man to marry a woman, he must in effect marry her family as well. In fact, both families must integrate; must become almost a part of each other. Thus, when two people live together it is the merging of two families. The families do not share each other's physical homes, but they do in essence become as one. Divorce is almost unknown.'

'Will you and Etan marry?'

'Our families were in the process of merging,' she said. 'Now, things are altered somewhat, but not changed entirely. We certainly will marry on the return journey.'

'I wish you well,' Austin said.

'Thank you ... You know, I do so miss the stars of home. They look very different in our skies. The galaxy looks much the same as it does from here, but the rest of the stars are entirely different. The other night, before you found us, I lay beneath some pine trees and looked at the stars. I looked for Tau Ceti and, you know, I couldn't find it. I tried for a long time, but it was no use.'

'It's fairly hard to find,' Austin said. 'You would really

have to know where to look.'

'I should have guessed that. Oddly enough, when I was home I had no trouble finding your star. But then, my whole life has been your star, your planet, your history, your language. It may strike you as funny, but I think I know more about your planet than I do about mine.'

'That *is* interesting.'

'But then, your planet has become, as you say, a cause célèbre on Cetus. It was the most amazing thing. Ever since we first picked up your radio signals, some fifty years ago, my people have been absolutely *fascinated* with the goings-on here. We have not only studied you, written the equivalent of doctoral dissertations on you, but followed your history as if it were a play, or theater. I cannot understate how popular you are on Cetus. We have watched your wars as if they were ours. We have suffered with you, and laughed with you, and all the time . . .'

'We had no idea,' Austin said. 'We thought we were alone.'

'Then, when the first television signals came through, there was jubilation. Before you developed television, we could only guess at what you looked like. Of course, we knew you were hominoid, but the specifics were denied us.'

'Was there one thing that prompted you to begin the journey?'

'Two things. Getting our first look at you, and noting your survival of the first five years of your nuclear age. When we departed Cetus we were receiving signals broadcast here in 1950. Of course, the time lag shortened as we came closer, so by the time we approached your solar system we were picking up broadcasts only a few minutes old.'

Austin laughed.

'What's funny?' she asked.

'Somehow, the thought of our first extraterrestrial contact judging us entirely by our television programs amuses me,' he said.

'I hope you will get the chance to meet Etan. The two of you seem to have become the most important people in my life.'

'I'd like that.'

'He'll be jealous of you, of course. He is small, and you are big. To him, you will seem immense, and that is without regarding your bionic strength.'

'But you *all* are small,' Austin protested.

'True. The women average five-foot-two, and the men five-foot-six. There is not much variation.'

'It is because your planet is half the size of ours. Certainly that is not Etan's fault.'

'No, but nonetheless it will bother him. There is a strong warrior tradition among our males, though, considering the rapid pace of our evolution, it is only a tradition. We have not had need of warriors in more than two centuries. My brother, Eymon, was selected to be guard for this expedition, and he received the ancient warrior training. It was a great honor for him, as it was an honor for me to have been selected the first Cetian to meet a member of another civilization. We both became ... I think you use the word *celebrities*.'

'I understand entirely. I received some notoriety myself as a result of having traveled to the moon.'

'And you have received honor for being a warrior?'

'No. It's a secret.'

'Nonetheless,' she said, 'you and my brother, you are two of a kind. You are both unique in your worlds, and you both are warriors.'

'I'm not much of a warrior,' Austin said.

'Nonsense. Eymon thought very highly of you.'

'Did he? Hey, wait a minute!' Austin exclaimed, fumbling through the folds of his pressure suit. In a small pocket, he located the bright metal disc the Cetian had given him back in the forest. Austin held it up and gazed at it, and as the sun hit it the disc glowed with a distinctive blue fire. Minonee stared at it with anguish that seemed nearly heart-rending.

'Your brother gave this to me,' Austin said. 'I don't know what it is.'

Minonee remained speechless for several of the longest seconds Austin had ever known, then with a plaintive cry she buried her face in her hands and began to sob.

Rudy Wells reached instinctively for her.

'Don't touch her!' Austin yelled, caressing her shoulder with his bionic hand. 'Minonee ... what's the matter?' he asked. When no answer was forthcoming, he took one of her hands in his and squeezed it. 'Minonee, please, tell me.'

After a minute she raised her face and rubbed the tears from her eyes. Austin gave her hand another little squeeze. She sighed deeply, took the disc from his hand, and held it tightly in her palm.

'He gave you his Warrior Ikon,' she said quietly.

Austin gave her a quizzical glance.

'Deep in our traditions are several spiritual symbols, and this is the most sacred one,' she said. 'When a warrior departed for a battle from which he knew he would not return, he gave his Ikon to his closest friend. It was a way of passing his ... spirit ... to his friend, so that it might continue after his death.'

It was Austin's turn to be speechless.

'Eymon was the last warrior of Cetus,' she said, 'and now he is you. Never again in your life will you be simply a Terran.' She gave the disc back to him. He tried to make her keep it, but she insisted that it remain his. Finally he reinserted the disc in his pocket.

'I don't know what to say,' he stammered.

'Nothing is necessary.'

'I'll never forget either of you.'

'You'll not be able to,' she said. 'Now that you are one of us.'

There was within the Shuttle absolute silence for ten minutes or more, until Copilot McCarthy, who had been handling countdown checkouts while Austin talked to the girl, motioned for Austin's attention.

'You'd better be in on this, Steve,' he said, flicking a switch which shifted capsule communications from his headset onto the cockpit monitors.

'What's up?' he asked.

'CAPCOM has received a communication on the Cetus frequency,' he said.

'It is from my people!' Minonee said joyfully.

Austin brought his communicator to his lips. 'Rescue to Kennedy,' he said.

'Rescue, this is Kennedy. Al McCall here.'

'What have you got, Al?'

'Steve, five minutes ago we received a message on the special frequency. We have it on tape. Are you ready to copy?'

'Ready,' Austin said.

The cockpit monitors bore forth a voice which sounded strange, wispy, and faroff, yet it spoke with the official ease of any NASA communications officer.

'Request permission to speak on this frequency on a matter of extreme importance,' it said.

'Etan!' the girl cried.

'Request received and acknowledged,' it said. 'Please be informed that *Cetus One* will comply. Estimated time of arrival: 0700 Saturday. Regards to Ambassador.'

'That's all of it, Steve,' McCall said.

'That's more than enough,' he replied.

Austin smiled at the girl, who was gazing skyward with a look of beatific happiness. 'I'm going home,' she said.

CHAPTER TEN

At precisely 10:01:27 the Shuttle rose from the midst of a swirling cloud of steam and fumes, lifted straight up into the morning air, then curved gently off to the east. As hundreds of journalists and more than a million other spectators watched in awe, the huge, four-part vehicle, appearing many times larger than any previous American rocket, disappeared into the perfectly clear sky.

A score miles high and halfway to Bermuda, computer switching initiated the jettison sequence for the two solid-fuel boosters; five miles farther from the earth's surface, explosive bolts blew the boosters to either side, and they peeled away from the Shuttle. Far below, two U.S. Navy destroyers mobilized their hastily briefed crews for the recovery of the boosters, which a minute after jettison were drifting idly toward the warm waters of the Gulf Stream, three parachutes managing the descent of each. Seven minutes later, the omniscient NASA launch computer signaled the jettison of the huge external fuel tank, which then fell away from the Shuttle and burned up in the atmosphere above the island of Maderia, off the North African coast.

The external tank was Rescue's last tie with ungainliness. Without its weight and bulk, the Shuttle assumed the form of a beautiful red-white-and-blue bird. Rescue achieved orbital insertion over the Atlas Mountains of Morocco, which lay beneath the craft like a string of delicate brown pebbles. Once in orbit and free of the relentless gravity of Earth, Austin felt an exhilaration which was long lost but fondly remembered. Five years had passed since he last broke free of gravity. Several short, suborbital flights had taken place, one of which was nearly his last.

In the years which had passed since that ominous day in the M3F5 shuttle prototype, Austin had been away from active space duty, playing the unfamiliar role of international operative. During those years he had to comfort him only the knowledge that the M3F5 disaster which resulted in his becoming a cyborg was also the cause of the design changes which resulted in the completed Shuttle he flew today.

What he knew as a snub-nosed, wingless bullet with a small tail assembly grew longer, slimmer, and more graceful. It sprouted large wings which extended back from cockpit to tail in a wide delta. It resembled a slightly overweight fighter-bomber, not at all an unpleasant design. As the craft moved smoothly over the southern shore of the Mediterranean, Austin activated manual control and tried some maneuvers. Moving at just under seventeen thousand miles per hour, an incredible speed for a winged craft but no problem in airless space, Austin flew Rescue as smoothly as he might a Piper Cub on a balmy Sunday afternoon. With no engine sound, no weight, and no rush of air past the window, the huge astronautical ambulance swooped, soared, waggled its wings, raised and lowered its nose, tried bogus docking approaches, and ran through every imaginable check of systems for two full orbits. If there is such a thing as a popular conception of space maneuvering, it is that such feats are extremely difficult. Actually, docking in space is a great deal more simple than, for example, coupling a B-52 bomber to its airborne fueling apparatus. In that latter situation, air pressure, gravity, and the possibility of running into something add three very real variables which do not exist in space. In space, the target vehicle isn't going anywhere and isn't likely to run into a mountain. One can take as much time as one likes in approaching it.

The problem Austin faced in completing the rescue of *Athena One* was not one of docking. If *Athena One*'s damaged maneuvering jets prevented Kelly Wood from making the approach with her small capsule, Austin could easily approach in the much larger shuttle. The problem was that, once docked, the docking hatch on *Athena* could not be opened through normal procedures. Austin would have to force it, but do so without breaking the vacuum seal between *Athena* and Rescue. Austin, Wells, McCarthy, Kelly, and Minonee would all be suited up. But the injured Osterman could not be put into his pressure suit, which had been torn up by flying metal anyway. A break in the vacuum seal would be fatal to him. In essence, Austin would have to hold the two vessels together with his arm while forcing the hatch with his legs, not an enviable task but no harder than some things he had done.

It was just two in the afternoon when Austin brought the craft to within visual range of *Athena*. The capsule lay in space a hundred yards from Skylab B, America's second space station, which had been fired into an equatorial orbit late in 1976 to replace Skylab A, which had lost part of its micrometeorite shield and a good deal of its solar array during launch early in 1973. Austin eased the shuttle toward the strange meeting of space vessels, and was half a mile from it when the cockpit monitors crackled and came alive.

'*Athena One* to Rescue.'

'Rescue,' Austin said.

'Welcome to the camp, Steve.'

'Glad to be here, Kelly. How's your partner.'

'Stable. But we'd better do something soon.'

'Rudy and I have a few things in mind. But let's get

docking over with first.'

'You're the boss.'

'What is your situation regarding maneuverability?'

'Are you kidding? For the past couple of hours I've had nothing better to do than fly docking passes with Skylab. Steve, the new guidance system is everything it's cracked up to be. *Athena* handles perfectly, even with one jet out.'

'Well, that at least will give them something to be happy about down on the ground. I'll hold Rescue here. You just come on in.'

'Right, Steve, and I promise – no gimbal lock this time.'

'You're on, Kelly,' Austin said, turning to his cockpit companions and pushing the mike from his lips.

'Ed and I are going to suit up in case of a pressure loss, Rudy. You and Minanee may as well sit in the cargo bay with the cockpit hatch closed. No sense in everybody having to suit up.'

'Can we be of any help here, Steve?' Wells asked.

'Nope.'

'Well then, Miss Ambassador,' Wells said, 'step into my office. I've been dying to do something with you.'

'I beg your pardon?' the girl exclaimed.

'I want to run some tests,' Wells said hurriedly, unstrapping himself from the gravity seat.

The pressurized module in which sat the cockpit of the Shuttle was connected via a large airlock to the huge cargo bay. The bay had two long doors which opened laterally, much as if someone sliced a pea pod down the middle and pulled apart the skin. The bay could be pressurized, and was for the mission which ground controllers had appropriately dubbed Rescue. Rudy Wells took the girl into the impromptu operating room created on the floor of the cargo bay and had her strip and recline on the pallet. For half an hour, while Austin and McCarthy worked behind the closed airlock, he ran an exhaustive series of tests, returning the information to the NASA computer by means of medical telemetry. When he was done, she slipped into her flight suit and accompanied the Terran doctor back to the cockpit.

Wells swung open the airlock, so filled with exhilaration he failed to notice that, docking completed, Kelly Wood had entered Rescue through the nose hatch.

'Steve!' Wells said. 'It's incredible. Her skin is covered with a secretion which is a kind of natural plastic! It's an ultraviolet shield! Apparently her planet's atmosphere has no ozone layer, and ...'

Kelly Wood stared at Minonee.

'What in God's name is this?' she asked.

Austin cleared his throat and took the lady astronaut by the arm.

'Kelly, this woman's name is Minonee. She is a visitor from a planet circling a nearby star ...'

'Steve,' Kelly said, 'I just got used to you knocking open that door as if it were a peanut. I'm afraid you're going to have to give me some time on this one.'

'I would be glad to explain,' Minonee said. 'I have a little speech rehearsed which gives the basic information.'

She beckoned the Terran woman to follow her into the cargo bay.

'What about Osterman?' Kelly protested.

'We'll bring him in,' Austin said. 'I think you realize I'm capable of handling it.'

'I guess so,' she said numbly, and followed the Cetian through the airlock.

'Steve, that woman is the most incredible product of evolution I've ever seen,' Rudy Wells said.

'I know.'

'Her internal organs have all the good of ours and none of the bad. Her nervous system acts like a sensitive radio transmitter and receiver ...'

'Rudy, I know ...'

'You just can't understand. I know some evolutionists who would *die* to get their hands on her.'

'That's exactly what they would do,' Austin said. 'Now, Doctor, you have a patient.'

'All right, all right,' Wells said, struggling to clear his mind of the heady thoughts.

'The docking seal is secure,' Austin continued. 'The door just required a little pressure. It was no big deal. As much as I hate to admit it, any healthy male could have done it.'

'Are you arguing against woman astronauts?' Wells smiled.

'Who, me? Come on, into the capsule. You have a look at him and tell me if it's okay to move him. If so, I'll bring him into the Shuttle.'

Wells nodded and allowed McCarthy to show him how to go through the docking hatch, located amid a cluttered technical area beneath and in front of the cockpit console.

Five minutes later, Wells reappeared in Rescue.

'Osterman is okay,' he said. 'Moving him won't hurt him. You know, this lack of gravity may be the best thing that ever happened to surgery.'

'I had the feeling it might be,' Austin said.

'When you move him, try not to constrict his abdomen or do anything which might bring forces to bear on the region of the heart.'

'Understood, Doctor. I'll go in and push him out to you. Remember that only minimal force is needed to move him around. Forget he's a full-grown man. Imagine him as a feather.'

'I'll try. Up here, you have the advantage over me.'

'It's about time,' Austin said, floating down toward the docking hatch.

Rescue and the much smaller *Athena* were clasped, nose

to nose, in the stillness of space, where even the most immense occurrences were silent and, hence, more portentous. Though the joined vessels whirled about Earth at approximately 17,000 miles per hour, completing an orbit every 91·6 minutes, no feeling of motion was experienced. Austin felt about him an eerie nothingness which made a stunning contrast to the beauty of Earth, below. He knew that after a few hours he would lose touch with the wonderment of it all, and what started out as a scientific marvel would become a routine mission. He intended to enjoy it for as long as he could. There was a good chance that it would be his last trip into space; as economic problems on Earth had forced cancellation of many NASA projects, younger astronauts were competing vigorously for the few available positions, and Oscar Goldman was perpetually demanding his services elsewhere, in earthbound endeavors. Well, he thought, there is no point in regretting the loss of what one has enjoyed immensely. Everything, even life itself, is transitory.

Austin entered the *Athena One* module, released Osterman from the straps which bound him, and guided his body, feet first, through the hatch. Wells and McCarthy took the injured man and brought him into the Shuttle's cargo bay, where Osterman was strapped to the pallet. After a minute Austin joined the group of people hovering around the medical facility.

'What time is it, Steve?' Wells asked.

'Uh . . . four o'clock,' Austin said.

'And *Cetus One* will be here . . .'

'Seven A.M. tomorrow. That gives us fifteen hours to wait. What do you want to do?'

'I can keep him stable for that long without problems, especially in the zero-G environment.'

'Do you have anything to do to keep you busy?' Austin asked.

'Well,' Rudy said, 'I can play around with Minonee some more . . . if she doesn't mind.'

'Not at all,' the Cetian said. 'Make your tests. That was one possibility we considered well.'

'I want to turn the medical scanner on her and have her do some of her parlor tricks,' Wells said. 'I'd like to see what changes occur in her nervous system.'

'Fine with me,' the girl said.

'Then it's settled,' Austin said. 'You two will do your tests and keep an eye on Osterman. Ed will watch the store. Kelly and I will suit up and do our EVA. We'll set up the orbiting astronomical telescope and do the other things we have to do in Skylab.'

Austin and Major Wood pressurized their suits and pushed their way into *Athena One*. Once inside, McCarthy closed the Shuttle hatch, repressurized the Shuttle cabin, and sat down to watch the EVA through the wide cockpit windows. Austin clambered into the co-pilot's station in *Athena*, allowing Kelly to take the driver's seat. She did so, and after the proper test of equipment and check with KSC, they blew *Athena* away from the Shuttle and took it to a position fifty yards distant.

With Austin supervising, she performed smoothly the tasks originally scheduled for her. She separated the command and service modules from the twenty-eight-foot cylinder which was modified from the old lunar module adapters. She brought the nose of the command module to it, and extracted from the adapter the orbiting astronomical telescope. Pushing the large optical telescope in front of her, she maneuvred *Athena* to within twenty feet of Skylab B. Then, while Kelly kept the capsule and Skylab at a static distance, Austin went outside, took the telescope, and attached it by hand to the Apollo Telescope Mount, located at the crux of the four-bladed solar array which looked ever so much like a windmill. After attaching both the telescope supports and the electrical connections, Austin floated back to *Athena* to collect his female partner. Together they powered down the *Athena* capsule and abandoned it, leaving it to drift slowly away from Skylab, eventually to return to Earth's atmosphere and incinerate itself.

Hand in hand, the two astronauts tumbled end-over-end toward Skylab. They worked their way along the body of that vessel, past the four-bladed ATM to the Multiple Docking Adapter. While Rescue floated a hundred yards to the port side, Austin and Wood entered Skylab's docking adapter hatch and closed it behind them. Five minutes later, the space station was powered up and pressurized, and the two astronauts were peeling off their pressure suits.

Skylab B was, in basic configuration, a duplicate of Skylab A. The overall size of a three-bedroom house, it consisted of four parts: the Orbital Workshop Stage (OWS), Airlock Module (AM), Multiply Docking Adapter (MDA), and Apollo Telescope Mount (ATM). The workshop contained ten thousand cubic feet of space and was forty-eight feet long by twenty-two feet wide. Within it were crew quarters and biomedical and engineering equipment. A long, fat tube, the workshop comprised the great bulk of the station.

Through a hatch, one traveled from the workshop to the Airlock Module, a pressurized passageway between OWS and MDA. It contained the station's life-support and power systems, and was seventeen feet long. The Multiple Docking Adapter provided two docking ports for command modules and the Shuttle, plus working space for the Apollo Telescope Mount. Like the AM, it was seventeen feet long. From it sprang the windmill-like solar array, which provided so much of the station's power.

After Austin shed his pressure suit he went to the Multiple Docking Adapter and, in communication with KSC, activated the telescope he had so recently installed.

For the next hour, he and the NASA computer worked out the kinks in the telescope guidance systems, finally getting it refined to the point where a mere six-digit instruction on a console would bring into focus any point in the visible universe, and a two-digit additional instruction would activate various filters to bring into play certain normally invisible portions of the universe.

For a time he amused himself by punching up the coordinates for Tau Ceti, observing that body on the closed-circuit monitor, and snapped a Polaroid photo of it. After the snapshot was fixed he slipped it into a pocket and returned the telescope to telemetry control. As he pushed his way into the living quarters he saw Kelly Wood sitting quietly in the astronaut maneuvering unit, a self-propelled chair.

'You look rather pensive,' he said, tumbling jauntily down the inside of the long, fat tube toward the food lockers.

She made no reply, so Austin rummaged about in one of the lockers until he located several small plastic squeeze tubes. He flipped one across the room to her, then stretched out in the air before her.

'What's this?' she asked, holding up the packet.

'B and B,' he said. 'Rather nice of them to think of it, wouldn't you say? You seem to need a drink.'

'I do,' she said quietly, ripping off the plastic tab and squeezing a small amount of the brandy onto her tongue.

'Anything I can help you with?' he asked.

'I just don't believe it, that's all.'

'Don't believe what?'

'It. The whole thing. Being in space, and that girl.'

'Yes,' Austin agreed, 'I can see where it is a bit harder to swallow than anything I expected.'

'Steve, is there really a ship coming to rendezvous with us? Is there really a *Cetus One*?'

'It would appear that way. I've grown accustomed to believing Minonee.'

'And the ship really is big?'

'Huge.'

The girl shrugged and finished her brandy.

'Got another of those?' she asked.

'It's against the rules of the house,' he smiled. 'It's not in the book.'

'What is?' she asked, shrugging. Unable to argue against that statement, he flipped her another packet, and took a second for himself.

He sipped at it and looked pensively at the array of scientific equipment surrounding them.

'I guess we'll have to rewrite the book after today,' he said.

'A lot of books will be rewritten,' she said, pushing herself from the chair and floating idly around the living quarters. 'How much time is there before we have to do anything?'

'It's seven now,' Austin said. '*Cetus One* is due to arrive in twelve hours. That gives us eight ...'

'In which to do absolutely nothing.'

'Actually, I thought you might like to get some sleep,' he said.

'Are you inviting me to bed, Colonel Austin?' she asked impishly.

'I would,' he said, 'if I had a bed.'

'Thoughtless of them to neglect it,' she said, 'especially after leaving all that B and B lying around and providing such a beautiful, Earthlit night.'

'Then of course there's medical telemetry,' Austin said, halfheartedly trying to scotch the idea.

'Telemetry isn't plugged in,' she said.

'There's a lot of sharp corners around here,' he said. 'One sneeze and you're across the room.'

'The sleeping quarters are nicely padded,' she said, pulling him against her and kissing him softly on the side of the neck.

'The idea does have some merit,' Austin said.

'Doesn't it?'

'I suppose,' he said, 'that in a way we would be idiots not to.'

'Just what I was thinking,' she whispered into his ear. 'You know, "one small step for man." '

Austin shrugged and allowed himself to be towed across the workshop toward the lower quarters, in which were the sleeping bags.

'Eat your heart out, Neil Armstrong,' he mumbled.

CHAPTER ELEVEN

Astronauts Austin and Wood awoke at three in the morning, bathed, and ate a breakfast squeezed from plastic tubes. Austin shaved, and the two of them pushed, pulled, and shoved their way into their pressure suits. After a final check of the newly installed telescope, they watched while Rescue copilot McCarthy guided the Shuttle to a perfect docking with Skylab. Then Austin and the girl climbed through the docking hatch into Rescue, leaving Skylab to be powered down by radio command from the ground. With Austin once again at the controls, Rescue pulled away from the space station, and, with a few slight bursts from its maneuvering jets, moved into position one half mile to the space side of Skylab, there to await the arrival of *Cetus One.*

The wait was not too long. At five in the morning, as Rescue drifted lazily over a thousand-mile whirlpool of stately rain clouds centered atop Madagascar, Austin was reclining in the pilot's seat, sipping a tubeful of coffee. The Shuttle windshield consisted of eight panes which wrapped around the cockpit area in a deep, U-shaped configuration. Austin was staring idly in the direction of the ecliptic, that imaginary line representing the plan in which most of the planetary orbits are located.

Suddenly, halfway between Regulus and Procyon, there appeared an object which was not there a few minutes earlier. Austin blinked, rubbed his eyes, and put aside the coffee. The object was larger than it was when he first saw it, at least twice as large. Austin scrambled for a locker and withdrew from it one of NASA's Hasselblads, equipped with motor drive, nine hundred frames worth of Ektachrome, and a 400mm telephoto.

'What's up?' Ed McCarthy asked.

'I think someone is coming to call,' Austin said. 'Tell the others.'

Austin focused the camera on the object, which was silver blue and had become the apparent size of Mars. He snapped a few frames, noted the arrival about him of the other Shuttle passengers, and, when he returned his attention to the camera, found that the object now was the apparent size of M31, the Adromeda Galaxy. 'My God,' he whispered, 'look at that damned thing move!'

'It's *Cetus One*,' Minonee said joyfully.

'What kind of machine can accelerate like that?' McCarthy wondered.

'Actually, by now it is decelerating,' Minonee said. 'One doesn't slow down from nearly the speed of light so rapidly.'

'I guess it isn't like slamming on the brakes,' Austin said.

'Steve, your capacity for understatement knows no bounds,' Rudy Wells commented.

Cetus One was the apparent size of the sun and growing with frightening rapidity. Austin clicked off several dozen shots of it, then put away the camera.

'How big is that thing?' Kelly asked.

'In diameter,' Minonee said, 'it is approximately one of your miles.'

'But that's only an approximation,' Austin said, smiling.

Cetus One had grown to a size which looked, to the Shuttle occupants, larger than the moon.

'Am I expected to contact it?' Austin asked.

'No. Too many radio communications will alert your

people, an occurrence you wish to avoid. The ship will take care of things. If I'm not mistaken, it will move into orbit near us, then draw us to it. Docking will be handled by my people.'

'They've had the time to make an adapter.'

'Lord yes,' she said, 'they've had time to make a dozen.'

'There's something I've been meaning to ask you,' Austin said. 'Why is it you have a slight British accent?'

Minonee blushed and looked away.

'Did I say something wrong?' he asked.

'No,' she said, smiling sheepishly. 'But I *was* warned about that by my tutors. For my language lessons I used to listen mainly to the BBC.'

'I had a feeling you wouldn't know who Captain Video was,' Austin said.

'You're right,' she said, 'I don't. But would you like to know the results of the last Test Matches?'

'I beg your pardon?'

'Cricket,' she said.

'God help us,' Austin said. 'The first visitors from another planet and they turn out to be Anglophiles. Next thing, we'll all be eating steak-and-kidney pie and riding to hounds.'

Cetus One appeared larger than the moon and twice as bright. Austin took the camera and snapped another series of shots.

'You're not doing something weird to the film, are you?' he asked. 'I would hate to be wasting all this high-speed Ektachrome.'

'No. You are welcome to your photographs. However, we are blocking radar and ground-based visual contact.'

'How is that possible?' he asked.

'I don't know any more than you do,' she said, 'only that it is done.'

Austin picked up the microphone and pressed some buttons. 'Rescue to Kennedy.'

'Kennedy. This is Al McCall.'

'Al, we have a clear visual on that 7 A.M. ETA. It's coming in early. Do you have anything?'

'Not a thing, Steve, no visual, no radar. Are you sure?'

'Couldn't be surer.'

'What is the approximate size?'

'About one mile in diameter.'

Al McCall's voice sounded exasperated. 'Are you serious?' he said. 'Nothing. Nothing at all down here.'

'Okay, Al. Receipt of your visual and radar is experiencing interference. I just wanted you to know that Rudy will be operating soon.'

'Fine, Steve,' McCall said. 'Give my best to his assistants.'

'Will do, Al,' Austin said, then switched off the transceiver.'

Cetus One approached slowly, moving into an orbit ahead of Rescue, then allowing Rescue to catch up with it. The crew members of Rescue stared at the ship silently. As they were drawn to it, it seemed more like a planetoid than a vessel. With its one-mile width, it seemed to stretch endlessly in either direction.

Cetus One was perfectly round, its smooth configuration marred only by a series of small maneuvring jets not unlike those used by NASA. The basic bluish-white color which permeated so much of the Cetian's life remained, even on the many small and large windows. Apparently the Cetians had found a window material which withstood the rigors of space, and as such could 'open' a lot more of their spacecraft than could the Terrans. The only major break in the spherical configuration was a large tunnel, fifty feet in diameter, which extended through the ship from front to back. Austin thought it was a docking facility and that Rescue would be drawn into it. But it turned out to be part of the propulsion system, and Rescue was drawn instead to an area on the starboard side of the huge vessel. As he watched in fascination, Rescue slid effortlessly up to the skin of the ship and docked just beneath a gigantic painted symbol, alien to Austin but quite obviously the Cetian equivalent of the NASA emblem which adorned Rescue's tail assembly.

'You're excited,' Austin said to Minonee.

'Yes. Etan is just inside.'

'Well then, one last request?'

'What?'

'May I touch you one more time before your lover comes in here and starts throwing rocks at me?'

She smiled. 'Yes,' she said, 'please.'

Using his bionic arm, Austin touched her cheek, then squeezed her hand. 'Thank you,' he said, 'for everything.'

'What have I done but cause you trouble?' she asked.

'The "thank you,"' he said, 'was for allowing me to see the future.'

Minonee looked up toward *Cetus One*, which dominated the Shuttle's windshield. After a second she returned her gaze to Austin.

'They would like you to open the hatch,' she said.

Austin pulled himself under the console and up to the hatch, located in the extreme nose of Rescue. A few quick turns on the wheel and the hatch opened inward. Through it came three Cetians, two dressed in the metallic blue flight suits, one dressed in yellow. Upon seeing them Minonee let out a small yelp and fell into the arms of one. They hugged each other for a long time, then she broke away and turned to face Austin.

'This is Etan,' she said. 'May I present Colonel Austin.'

'Colonel,' Etan said, extending his hand and allowing Austin to grasp it. 'I want to thank you for saving her.'

'And I want to thank you for offering to help our injured

man. I'm only sorry I couldn't have saved Minonee's family.'

The two Cetians smiled, then Minonee turned her concentration to more important matters. She indicated the other two Cetians, and introduced them as Arco, a surgeon, and Uru, an anesthesiologist. Austin in turn introduced them to Rudy Wells, who led them off into the operating facility.

'I will have to go with them to translate,' Minonee said. 'In the meantime, I'm afraid I must prevail upon you once again.'

'Anything.'

'You and Commander Wood must accompany Etan. He will take you into *Cetus One*, where several of our doctors would like, as you say, to run some tests.'

'I may not be the most typical speciman of Terran life,' Austin said.

'We know that,' she said. 'That is why Miss Wood should accompany you. She is typical enough. You are representative of the most advanced stages of your medical technology. I hope the two of you won't mind being, as you say, guinea pigs. After all, now that you are intimate . . .'

'Excuse me?' Kelly asked.

'Neither of you said a word, but I found out nonetheless. I think it's charming. Your ardor is very . . .'

'Human?' Austin asked.

'Understandable,' she said. 'It's too bad the act doesn't mean more in your society. You seem well suited for each other.'

'I think she's proposing for you,' Kelly said.

'I think I'll settle for being a guinea pig,' Austin replied, taking Kelly by the hand and leading her toward the docking hatch.

'If I wasn't so lovable, I'd kick your ass for that crack,' she said.

Austin took her by the hips and shoved her through the hatch. She spun out into a large room filled with Cetian technicians. Austin and Etan followed her.

'Prepare yourselves,' Etan said. 'We are switching on the gravity in this room.'

'Okay.' A second later Austin found his feet on the floor for the first time in a day. He helped Kelly find her balance, then looked around. The room was plain, even ordinary, decorated with color photographs of Cetus. Austin inspected them silently, but as they revealed to the naked eye no more than is revealed by the *Apollo* moon photos of Earth, he soon lost interest and stared instead at a battery of electronic equipment filling one wall.

'Can you show me more of the ship?' Austin asked.

'I'm afraid not. Our council met and decided it was best to limit your exposure to one room. It is not a matter of security, nor a matter of your learning too much. Cetian technology is, for the most part, restricted to Cetians.'

'I know. So much of it depends upon your ability to manipulate electromagnetic forces.'

'I see my lady has taught you well. Actually, we are worried about the effect of residual radiation on your bodies. This whole matter with the incompatibility of our systems is most distressing to us.'

'A few of my people are pretty bugged about it, too.'

'Anyway, if you and Commander Wood would please stand where you are and breathe normally, our instrument will scan you and make a record of your form and processes. It will take less than two of your minutes.'

'Agreed,' Austin said.

Kelly and he stood stock-still for the required time, until the Cetian signaled them to relax.

'I wish I could see more of the ship,' Austin said.

'I'm sorry. However,' the Cetian said, 'I can give you this.' He handed Austin several sheets of a plastic paper.

Upon the sheets were written a series of mathematical equations.

'What's this?'

'You were good enough to give us the agricultural information. In return, here is what you requested. The information on the guiding principle behind our ion drive. No doubt your scientists will understand it.'

'No doubt.'

'It really is quite simple. All you need is a sample of our irradiated metals, such as we use in our technical and ceremonial constructions, and you can figure it out.'

'And where am I to get that?' Austin asked.

'Again, I must apologize,' the Cetian said. 'I cannot give you a sample unless our council agrees to the cultural exchange ...'

'I would like to speak with the leader of your council,' Austin said.

'You have already done so,' Etan said, smiling.

'I have?'

'You saved her life.'

'Minonee is ...'

'The leader of *Cetus One*. That is correct.'

'Was I being discussed?' the girl said, sliding through the docking hatch, the two Cetian doctors close behind her.

'You didn't tell me you were the boss,' Austin said.

'You didn't ask.'

'Oh, for God's sake, Minonee.'

'You have everything you need, Steve,' she said. 'Including the health of your fellow astronaut. Major Osterman is now well enough to withstand re-entry. In one or two hours his scars will disappear entirely. In a day he will be as good as new.'

'And you? Do you have what you need?' Austin asked.

The Cetian turned serious, faced her people, and in Cetian asked them to leave. Silently the group of technicians followed Etan from the room. A sliding door sealed them off from the rest of the ship.

'Kelly?' Austin said.

The Terran woman smiled knowingly, patted Austin on the arm, and climbed back into the Shuttle.

Minonee stepped up to Austin and took him by the hand.

'It's been a long several days,' she said.

He nodded in agreement.

Minonee led him to a large mural of Cetus. She pointed out a small peninsula on the southern edge of the largest Cetian continent.

'There,' she said, 'Etan and I will make our home there. It is warm, with a soft breeze blowing in from the sea. Etan is fond of the sea, and I like the sound the waves make when they break upon the shore. We will have children, and . . .'

'If you say that you're going to name one after me, I swear I'll become ill,' Austin said.

She laughed. 'No,' she said, 'we couldn't do that. Your name would sound funny on my planet. Besides, it is a terrible cliché.'

'So is people from other planets,' Austin said.

'At least we didn't come as conquerors.'

'You aren't coming back, are you,' Austin said solemnly.

She thought for a long moment. 'I don't know. It really isn't entirely up to me. If it were, we would stay. But then, the reaction of your general population would be chaotic. You know that.'

'I know,' he said.

'I'm sorry, Steve.' She picked up his bionic hand, held it in her hand, and kissed the back of his fingers. Then she pressed the spot against his lips.

'That will have to do,' she said.

A small tear was forming in Austin's eye. He wiped it away and reached into his pocket for the Polariod snapshot of Tau Ceti. He handed it to her.

'A while back you said you looked at the stars and couldn't find home. Well, I found it for you.'

She smiled. 'Good-bye, Steve,' she said.

Austin tried to smile, but lost the gesture in the effort to hold back the tears. Finally he managed a slight smile and a shrug, then disappeared through the docking hatch. Inside, Rudy Wells was in a state of near ecstasy.

'Steve,' he shouted. 'They can do things we never *dreamed* of on Earth! One of them anesthetized Osterman just by holding his hands near him! The other one sealed up the incisions I made without touching them! They ...'

Austin had slumped into the pilot's seat.

'Rudy,' he interrupted, several large tears rolling down his cheeks.

'What?'

'Shut the hell up!'

Leaving those around him to stare silently, Austin cupped his face in his hands and began to weep.

CHAPTER TWELVE

Oscar Goldman sipped a cup of coffee while standing at the small bunker located at the northern end of the Shuttle runway which took up so much of Kennedy Space Center's 140,000 acres. Around him, two ambulances, several government station wagons, and the astronaut transport van waited for Rescue to return from its maiden flight.

As had been the case all week, the weather was annoying. The heat seemed to lie in the air like a hot, wet blanket, smothering all it touched. It was two in the afternoon, and a few small cumulus clouds were drifting lazily across the sky. Halfway through his coffee, Goldman gave the brown liquid an evil glance, poured it onto the grass, and tossed the empty container into a trash barrel.

'Where are they?' he mumbled to an aide, who was patched in to Launch Control by briefcase telephone.

'Seven hundred miles, sir,' the aide said, 'and thirty-six thousand two hundred thirty feet per second.'

'Where the hell is that?' Goldman snapped.

'Over the Gulf of Mexico and on perfect approach.'

'How long will it be?'

'Just a few minutes.'

'Is it hot here or is it me?' Goldman asked, mopping his brow with a meticulously folded handkerchief.

'It's hot here, Mr Goldman.'

'Well, that's one thing I can believe anyway,' he said.

'Sir?'

'Nothing. How long now?'

'Landing gear is down, sir.'

Goldman cupped his hand over his eyes and stared off toward the south, but the glare of the sun caught him, and he swore at it.

'Into the trench, sir,' the aide said.

'The trench?'

'The bunker, Mr Goldman. That bird is going to come in here like gangbusters, and we don't want to be in the way.'

Goldman nodded and complied, following the aide and several other ground technicians into the stark, concrete building.

'Who built this place, Urban Renewal?'

'It's just a bunker.'

'Is that the word for tragedy these days?'

'Please calm down, Mr Goldman, Colonel Austin is coming now.'

'Where?'

'Just listen, sir.'

Goldman cocked an ear to the south. Far off, but growing ominously closer, was a sound like that of a hundred bombers coming in for a run. Once again shielding his eyes, Goldman stared into the sky and, from a point in the heavens directly south of the Cape, there came a thunderous roar and a flotilla of wings. Rescue glided down from the sky, making no noise of its own, but surrounded by a bevy of fighter escorts and observation helicopters.

All across the Cape and KSC, thousands of persons leaned on their car horns. As Rescue eased into its final glide path, a squadron of fighters took off from the air force base and roared overhead in welcome. The millions lining the beach cheered and waved, and scores of photographers clicked scores of cameras. The Shuttle touched down with no more difficulty than is experienced by a 727 captain coming into Kennedy International airport. It ate up the four miles of runway in seconds, three gigantic red-white-and-blue parachutes, trailing behind, slowing it to a gentle roll and finally a complete halt.

As Goldmnn joined the flood of technicians racing across the runway to join the stilled Shuttle, Austin, who had said barely a word since *Cetus One* disengaged itself and sailed silently off into the galaxy, unhooked, unstrapped, and de-suited himself and turned over the console to copilot McCarthy. The parachutes were lying flat on the runway. The Shuttle would be towed back to the Vertical Assembly Building, where it would be raised and refitted for another flight. Osterman would be taken to the base hospital, where he would have to undergo the aggravation of pretending to be injured, lest the public marvel at his almost instantaneous recovery. And Kelly Wood was destined for celebration as the first woman astronaut. The battles had been won but, as happens now and then, the war was lost. Austin made his way to the exit bay and let himself out. Completely disregarding the stares of the technicians, he dropped ten feet to the ground and walked disgustedly off toward the front of the ship, which was pointed, quite ironically, into the heart of the Merritt Island National Wildlife Refuge.

Dozens of men busied themselves in the vicinity of the Shuttle, but only one of them, Oscar Goldman, had the nerve to approach Austin.

'Steve,' he yelled, jogging toward the nose of Rescue.

'Buzz off, Oscar,' Austin growled.

'Congratulations! You did it!'

'Did I?'

'Of course. Come on, let's go back to Launch Control. Al wants to talk to you.'

'Leave me alone, would you?'

'What's the matter?'

'The matter, Oscar,' Austin said, wheeling to face his antagonist, 'is that I'm gonna bust the first nose that gets stuck in my business.'

'What happened up there?'

'Nothing, Oscar,' he said, taking a wadded-up sheath of papers from his pocket and handing them to Goldman.

'What's this?'

'Your goddam ion drive.'

'That's great!'

'Wonderful.'

'What *is* the matter?'

'We blew it, Oscar, that's what the matter is. *They* blew it, those stupid idiots with their shotguns. I got half a mind to go out tonight and change their shirt sizes.'

'No, Steve, calm down. They didn't know.'

'Famous last words, Oscar. "They didn't know."'

'All right, all right,' Goldman said. 'Let's go.'

'I want to be alone.'

'Come on, we'll go out tonight and tie one on, how about that?'

'I'll consider it. In the meantime, get lost. I'm going to walk back.'

'Maybe it isn't blown. Maybe they'll decide for the cultural exchange. Maybe we *are* ... how did she put it ... ready to join the galaxy.'

'*We're* ready. You and I are ready. *They're* not,' Austin said, pointing toward the wildlife refuge. 'All they want to do is run around the woods and shoot things. Is this where five million years of evolution has brought us?'

'Okay, if you're going to be inconsolable, I'm not going to bother with you. Go ahead and walk back. I'll take this to the scientists and see you later.'

Goldman turned and walked off, expecting Austin to relent and join him. But when Goldman climbed into his car, Austin was still staring silently at the wildlife refuge, just beyond the end of the runway. After a moment Goldman shrugged and drove back to Launch Control.

When Austin finally walked into the firing room it was nearly five o'clock. Half the consoles were shut down, and the rest were operating with little supervision. The far part of the room was in darkness. In all, the array of not-in-use consoles gave the feeling of technology which had come to naught. A patch of light from one array of neon lamps illuminated Al McCall, Oscar Goldman, and Kelly Wood.

'Steve,' McCall said. 'Where have you been?'

'Out.'

'What have you been doing?'

'Nothing.'

'Steve, you know you're supposed to follow certain rules and procedures. Perhaps you've heard of debriefing?'

'I've said all I have to say,' Austin said sullenly.

'We still haven't heard from them, Steve,' Goldman said hopefully. 'They're just sitting there, back beyond the orbit of Jupiter, making up their minds.'

'Anyway, that formula you came up with is worth a mint,' McCall said. 'We pored over it, and it's the real thing! It's the breakthrough our boys have been waiting for! It's at least a hundred years in advance of any propulsion system we've ever *dreamed* about.'

'Now we can go to *them*,' Kelly said.

'If we had one thing,' McCall said.

'What's that?' Austin asked.

'A sample of their irradiated metal.'

'I know that. They wouldn't give me one. They said it's reserved for their technical and ceremonial constructions.'

'We've got a crew off Black Point trying to come up with the remains of their scout ship. As yet, we haven't found anything. I hope we do. Without a piece of their metal, the formula is worthless.'

'Without that, the ion drive is just an intriguing idea, that's all,' Goldman said.

'Well,' Austin shrugged, 'I guess that's that.'

'Message, sir,' a voice called.

'What?' McCall asked.

'Something is coming on the videocom.'

'Put it here,' McCall said.

'Switching to you,' the aide said.

Suddenly the monitor at McCall's station lit up.

'What's this?' Goldman asked.

'I don't know.'

McCall, Goldman, Austin, and Wood watched as the monitor flickered a few seconds, then printed out, in sterile computer-type, the following message:

AMBASSADOR TO FIDO . . .

'That's you, Steve,' Kelly said.

It seems a shame
The walrus said,
To play them such a trick.
After we've brought them out so far,
and made them trot so quick.

McCall stared incredulously at Goldman, who shrugged in disbelief.

'What the hell was that all about?' McCall asked.

Austin said nothing, but turned away from the group, walked to the wall, and stared at it in fury. Then, as all watched in horror, he cocked his fist and drove it through the wall, spraying the hall with concrete and plaster!

'Steve!' Goldman shouted.

Austin turned, faced them, and stared them into silence.

'That means good-bye,' Austin said.

'I don't understand,' Kelly said.

'They're going away,' Austin said, 'and probably they're

not coming back. Not for a long while, anyway.'

Silence reigned for fully five minutes before McCall found the courage to break it.

'Well, someday we'll go to them. It's inevitable. The Russians are *humming*. You should have seen the phone wires buzz this afternoon. They don't know what happened, but they suspect. Maybe if we toss this formula back and forth between us, we'll come up with something, even without a sample of their metal.'

'I'm going,' Austin said, as if he hadn't heard.

'I'll go with you,' Kelly said. Smiling politely, the two astronauts walked from the building and across the lawn toward the parking lot, where Austin's Mercedes remained.

The sun was pushing down toward the western horizon as Major Wood took Austin by the arm.

'I've got one hell of a steak I can fix up for us,' she said, 'and, you know what? I've got a bottle of wine you wouldn't believe. A Chateau Lafitte Rothschild '62. How about that?'

'What the hell,' Austin said without enthusiasm.

'Come on now, Colonel,' she said. 'Who gets invited to a girl's house twice in one day, both on and off Earth?'

'The stars will be out soon,' Austin said, gazing skyward at a small cloud.

Kelly stopped and stared at him.

'You have the most amazing ability to ignore what other people are saying,' she said.

'Look, lady!' Austin exploded. 'Do you realize that we just blew the first and perhaps the only contact between us and people from another star system! That's it, kid. We just crawl out of the tree, and the first time somebody says hello, we bop him on the head with a coconut!'

'I'm sorry, Steve.'

'Sorry isn't good enough.'

'Maybe we *can* develop an ion drive which would take us there.'

'In a hundred years,' Austin said venomously.

The girl took hold of his arm and squeezed it. 'Unless . . .' he said, his face suddenly turning from despair to realization.

'Unless what?' Kelly asked, pushing away from him.

'Unless we have a sample of their metal.'

Austin fumbled through his pockets until he found the Warrior Ikon. He stared at it and held it up to the sun until the stream of solar photons made it glow a fiery blue. It was alive. It seemed to pulse with energy.

'What's that?' she asked.

Austin stared at the medal in reverent silence.

'We've got to talk to Al McCall. I think he's going to want to see this.'

'What is it?'

'A ticket to the stars,' he said, taking her by the hand and running her off toward the firing room.

SICILIAN DEFENCE
John Nicholas Iannuzzi

On a chessboard called New York City, blacks and whites clash in the biggest game in town – with the biggest stakes. A powerful Sicilian Don is snatched from the top of the New York crime scene. His lieutenants move out to snatch him back – with bribery, violence and corruption, the game begins. *50p*

OPERATION CASINO
Leo Rost

"Rost knows the passion and stench of big-time gambling . . . his suspense broods and smoulders and his people breathe and sweat. This is one hell of a yarn." DAVID MARKSON

A tale of corruption in the Bahamas where the stake is survival. *60p*

THE OVERLORDS
William Woolfolk

When the California Governor's plane crashed and one million dollars in cash was found hidden in his home, Steve Gifford, ex-FBI, tough, unrelenting, was given an assignment. A nightmare spreads to involve the two-faced masks of justice, law, even family and friends . . . and the Syndicate's plan becomes a little more specific – *get Gifford.* *75p*

THE TAKEOVER
Niven Busch

The fierce battlefield of politics versus law. Four men, all well on their way to becoming billionaires, pass a death sentence on a fifth – Jed, the President of their Corporation. Soon enough it's the White House itself that needs paying off . . . "As up to date as this morning's headline news. A fast-paced, spellbinding story, Niven Busch's finest book so far." ARTHUR HAILEY *50p*

COLUMBO

When TV launched Lieutenant Columbo before the eyes of the British public the seeds were sown for an all-time classic success. A cult has grown up around the short stooping man with unruly black hair, dressed in a dirty old raincoat and chewing the end of a cigar. Columbo is unique. And his special brand of investigation now makes spectacular reading. Alfred Lawrence has taken the TV series to its logical conclusion, a series of novels – thrillers which do perfect justice to the TV character played by Peter Falk. Have you read them?

THE DEAN'S DEATH
Alfred Lawrence

A CHRISTMAS KILLING
Alfred Lawrence

40p and 45p respectively

STAR BOOKS

are available through all good booksellers but, where difficulty is encountered, titles can usually be obtained *by post* from:

Star Book Service,
G.P.O. Box 29,
Douglas,
Isle of Man,
British Isles.

Please send retail price plus 8p per copy.

Customers outside the British Isles should include 10p post/packing per copy.

Book prices are subject to alteration without notice.